ANIMALS

in

CAPTIVITY

ANIMALS

in

CAPTIVITY

Kate Segriff

Riddle Fence Debuts
St. John's, NL

ANIMALS IN CAPTIVITY
Copyright © 2024 by Kate Segriff

Riddle Fence Publishing Inc.
PO Box 7092
St. John's, NL A1E 3Y3, Canada
www.riddlefence.com

The publisher gratefully acknowledges the support of the Canada Council for the Arts, the Newfoundland and Labrador Arts Council, and the Government of NL.

Canada Council   Conseil des arts
for the Arts   du Canada

Arts NL
NEWFOUNDLAND AND LABRADOR ARTS COUNCIL

Newfoundland
Labrador

Riddle Fence Publishing acknowledges the land on which we work as the ancestral homelands of the Beothuk, whose culture has now been erased forever. We also acknowledge the island of Ktaqmkuk (Newfoundland) as the unceded, traditional territory of the Beothuk and the Mi'kmaq. And we acknowledge Labrador as the traditional and ancestral homelands of the Innu of Nitassinan, the Inuit of Nunatsiavut, and the Inuit of NunatuKavut.

This is a work of fiction. Any resemblance of characters to persons either living or deceased is purely coincidental.

Cover and text design by: Graham Blair
Cover art by: Darren Whalen, "Tongue Tied"
Edited by: Eva Crocker

Printed and bound in Canada

Library and Archives Canada Cataloguing in Publication
Title: Animals in captivity / Kate Segriff.
Names: Segriff, Kate, author.
Identifiers: Canadiana (print) 2023059039X | Canadiana (ebook) 20230590438 | ISBN 9781738151561 (softcover) | ISBN 9781738151578 (EPUB)
Subjects: LCGFT: Short stories.
Classification: LCC PS8637.E454 A83 2024 | DDC C813/.6—dc23

Contents

Animals in Captivity

Darlene watches me feed the hogs. I can tell she has something on her mind, but if she wants to say it, she can go ahead. I'm not going to spend my day trying to pull it out of her. She's in the wrong, she goddamn knows it, and the one who's deepest in the shitpile is the one who's got to start shovelling.

"Why you always gotta make things so difficult?" Darlene says.

"Wasn't me who pulled the rotten screw on a live grenade and then tossed it backward into our lives," I say. "Believe that was yours truly."

"Rotten screw, Char? That's fuckin' hilarious. Don't think I didn't catch it. You're calling me a slut."

"Your words, Dar, not mine. But you always were the smart one."

Darlene is my twin. Marni, our supposed cousin and sometimes hired hand, says that's in name only. Yesterday, Marni remarked, "Jesus, Charlene, how did a square face like yours pop out of the same hole as Darling Darlie?"

Marni's a skag, but you don't have to look twice to see the truth in what she says. I don't take offense. Marni's been working with us off and on for three years now, and that's been enough time for me to learn I'd have better luck milking a bull than getting a kind word out of her.

Darlene hops up on the fence with pep you wouldn't expect from someone who's seven months pregnant. I know she's trying to get some physical distance between the two of us before she lays whatever rotten egg she's incubating. Darlene and I have been swimming around together for twenty-eight years now, ever since we were duking it out for real estate in Mum's yoot, and anyone who tells you twins can't read each other's minds is selling you bullshit.

I hadn't realized I was lesbian until Darlene told me so. There's us, ten years old, in the stands of the smash-up derby with our dad, and Darlene leans over to me and whispers, "I know you're thinking about kissing Lucy Lawless."

Turns out I was.

Darlene presses her palms to the fence rails and says, "You're first to know, Charlie. I've decided to move in with Big Chip."

"Big Chip knows it?"

"Yeah."

"Then I'm not the first."

Darlene shoots me a foul look. "I ain't gonna sit and argue with you, Charlie, my mind's made up."

"Well, unmake it. It's the wrong decision."

I go back to feeding the hogs, and Darlene looks out over the field beyond the fence.

"Corn's about ready," she says.

I ignore her and keep scooping out the slop. The pigs shake their asses and fall over each other like they always do while they're stuffing their mouths. They're damn feral animals, if you want my opinion, but bacon's got to come from somewhere.

Darlene grabs one of the cornstalks, bends it toward her, and lets it go. I gather up my pails and start walking. I'm halfway to the barn when she jumps off the fence and starts to follow me.

"I ain't gonna be some trash baby-momma in the delivery room alone," she calls across the yard.

I pause for a moment to consider what she's peddling.

"So, you figure that the presence of Big Chip will add a certain sophistication to that situation?"

I understand how Darlene got to where she's at. Me and Dar have lived on this farm our whole lives, and, since Dad died, we've been running the bitch mostly on our own. So, I know a few things about animal needs. I might not personally understand how you can look at a sight as sore as Big Chip and feel like it's time to saddle up, but I appreciate that my tastes aren't what many would consider common. The way I see it, Darlene dove into a rotten pond when her heat was up and she needed to cool it. I don't fault her for that. What I fail to understand is why, once she came up for air and realized what a mess she was swimming in, she chose to put her head back under and drown.

"Big Chip ain't so bad," Darlene says.

I know what she means, even if I disagree with her. I don't think Big Chip has ever smacked Darlene or stolen any of her money. He's never been to jail, as far as I know. If you want to dig deep, he is a homeowner of sorts: he bought his trailer outright with the settlement he got from his back injury at the pit. Those facts alone put him miles above some of the skids around here, but they are hardly grounds for knighthood.

"He ain't so good neither," I reply.

Taken as a whole, Big Chip is a grade-A fuckhead. He sits in his trailer all day rolling joints and watching reality television. Half of what comes out of his mouth is cuss words, and the other half is bullshit. Even if he didn't call me a bull-dyke every time he saw me at Kool's Variety, I would still walk the other way whenever I saw him coming.

Darlene is supposed to be the brains of the operation – if she weren't around to do the taxes, Revenue Goddamn Canada would probably chew through us like a stick of stale jerky – so it chaps my ass she's found herself in such a bloody state. I also feel rotten for our near-ripe baby girl – who me and Darlene have already named Lexie – because she hasn't got a clue that her daddy is a sloppy shithead named Big Chip.

"Dar, Big Chip doesn't even know you're smart. He's probably never seen past your tits. He'll make a mess of you and Lex in the span of half a second. The only reason you don't know it is that you're too charged up with hormones to know a sweet peach from a rotten fig."

I look over at Darlene and can see from the set of her jaw that any further argument will only drive her deeper inside her hole. I decide to leave it.

"I'm going tomorrow tonight. You'll have to drive me," she says.

I've got nothing more to add, so I just let my breath whistle out from between my teeth.

Me and Darlene both startle when Marni pipes up behind us. That woman is like an inland taipan. She's got her teeth sunk in before you even know she's spotted you.

"Trouble in paradise, skanks?" Marni growls, her voice worn raw from fifteen solid years of smoking.

Darlene and I raise our middle fingers to Marni in unison, and it's nice to see we still agree on something. We should have gotten rid of Marni years ago for all the trouble she causes us, but she's a good worker, and I can count on three fingers the number of people in this county who know the definition of a solid day's work.

As I appear to be getting exactly nowhere with Darlene, I decide to take matters into my own hands and drive up to Big Chip's trailer to have a word.

I ease out of the Chevy and trudge up to the trailer window. Big Chip is stretched out in front of the television like a side-lying swine. He's watching that show where models get a chance to be porn stars and fall all over each other trying to out-trash the competition. He must have heard me coming up the lane, but he keeps his eyes locked on the tube. A gravel truck roars by on the road behind me, and Big Chip's eyes don't even flicker, so I know for sure the ass sees me. I hammer on the door, and, after a pause, Big Chip mutters.

"Okay. Charlene. Come in if you fuckin' insist."

When I enter the living room, I almost fall backward from the stench of old sweat and weed, and that's saying a lot for someone who spent the morning feeding hogs.

I get straight to it.

"You're planning to move my niece into this piece-of-shit trailer?"

We both survey the trailer's interior: its dirty carpet, taped-up window screens, and coffee table full of bongs and papers. I know Big Chip sees what I see, but either he chooses to ignore it, or he just doesn't care.

"You wanna live like an animal, you're welcome to it," I say. "But if you think you're dragging our Lexie through your trough, you better think thrice."

Big Chip heaves himself around a little, and I think he might stand, but then I realize he is just digging himself deeper into the couch pillows. I notice there's a baby doll sitting beside him, and I almost laugh. It's the plastic kind with the poorly painted-on eyes and cheap little buttons on its dress. It's something you might pick up at the dollar store if you'd never spent one hot minute alone with a baby and didn't know jack about all the things they can choke on.

"I don't know who the fuck Lexie is," he says, "but if you're talking about Darlene's baby, I'm gonna name her Cheryl, after my cousin."

Everyone in town knows Cheryl Chipchase died of an accidental overdose eight years ago even though the family tried to say it was a heart attack. I think the idea of naming a child after her is ass-backward – the kid's already got enough challenges in the ancestry department with Big Chip's name on her birth certificate – but I hold my peace.

"Darlene can't see a straight line because she's impaired by her condition," I say, "but what's your friggin' excuse? If you cared anything for the fetus that will shortly transform into your daughter, you would send Darlene packing until she comes to her senses and dumps you herself. As far as I'm concerned, that's the best gift you could give our baby girl."

Big Chip struggles up from the couch, gets right in my face, and says, "I guess if you were growing my kid in that ugly gut of yours, Charlene, it might be any of your fuckin' business, but since you aren't, why don't you eat shit and get off my property?"

There isn't much you can say to that without hitting a wall, so I leave.

I am too worked up to go home and scrap with Darlene again, so I go down to Willies for a drink. Cindy Constantine's Mustang is parked in the lot, and that means they'll be rolling the hair metal playlist so the lads can watch Cindy shake. I know Cindy from high school, and she bothers me less than most people do, so I'm not necessarily disappointed to see her car.

I enter the bar and head for my usual table by the fire exit. I like to sit there because, even in my best moods, I am not inclined to strike up a conversation with most of the jerk-offs in this town. Apart from the sparse words I occasionally share with Cindy, I'd be just as happy if the whole goddamn town was mute. It's not a particularly welcoming place for a woman like me, but the only thing my dad ever taught me was how to farm, so I haven't got a ton of other options.

I sit at my table, knock back a Jack's, and watch Cindy Constantine spin around on the dance floor in her acid-washed jeans to Vince Neil screeching that she's "Too fast for Love." A lot of folks say Cindy's trash, but there's something sort of elegant about the way she paints a figure eight with her hips.

The way Cindy moves gets me thinking. Cindy is known to

make a few extra dollars for the favours she grants to the locals. Also, and perhaps more importantly, I am pretty sure she used to hang around with Big Chip.

The next time Cindy slides herself against the bar, I cross the room and move in beside her.

"Hey, Cindy," I say, and she smiles up at me in a way most people in town don't.

"Hey, Charlie, you want a Mars bar?" She grabs one from behind the bar because she knows damn right that I do. They had a vending machine back in our high school, and between the two of us, I think me and Cindy pushed the Mars factory on Sheldon Street into the black.

"I need a favour," I say as I unwrap the bar and lick the already melted chocolate from my fingers. "And I'll pay you double your usual."

Cindy looks at me without blinking and says, "No offense, Charlie, but I don't do chicks. Not for cash, anyway."

"I didn't mean for me, you fuckin' freak show."

Cindy takes a swallow of her beer and waits. She's not one for chatting, which is a quality I admire.

"I need you to go up to the trailer tomorrow around six," I say, "and come on to Big Chip."

Cindy screws up her face, but I forge on. "You don't have to do him or anything," I say, "unless you want to. Just get him to chase you a bit, you know?"

"Why would you want me to do that?" Cindy says. "Ain't he movin' in with your sister, Darlene?"

So much for being the first to know.

"Yeah, Cin, and how do you think that's gonna end?"

"Big Chip ain't so bad."

Cindy and I stare at each other, and I wait for her to reconsider, which she does.

"No, you're right, Charlie. He's a piece of shit. Darlene should have got rid of that kid the moment she pissed positive."

"Well, she didn't, and now she's horny to play house with Big Chip, and I think someone's gotta set her straight before she takes my niece down with her. I don't think she even really likes him. Maybe it's just a grief thing since we lost our own dad so young."

"She having a girl?"

"Yeah. We already named her Lexie."

"No shit? That's a beaut name. Kinda name I'd give a girl if I had one. Not that I ever will."

"Why not? Seems like you've got lots of potential fathers."

Cindy rolls her eyes and snorts into her beer. She knows I don't mean it badly. Me and Cindy aren't friends exactly, but we've been razzing each other for a lot of years.

"You had the kind of mother and sister I did, you'd think twice about bringing any more women into this world."

I know it's not a pity party Cindy's throwing herself. Those are just the facts. The story of Cindy's early years would take most folks' breath away. Cindy wipes the froth from the edge of her glass and licks it like it's a dollop of fresh cream. I can guess where her mind has dropped off to, so I give her some space to climb back into the present.

"What's all this to do with me blue-balling Big Chip?" Cindy says after a few more swallows of her beer.

"I'm driving Darlene over to his place tomorrow night with her suitcase. So, I figured if she caught him in the act … "

Cindy passes her eyes around the bar and chews on that information. Every so often, she looks over at me and then looks away, and I realize she is going to refuse me. Then, out of nowhere, the full extent of my asshole plan slaps me hard across the face, and I feel unfit to walk the earth.

"You know what, Cindy. I'm sorry I asked you," I say. "Like not 'fuck-you sorry' but really sorry. It was a bullshit idea."

Cindy stares at her fingers and starts to pick non-existent dirt from beneath her cherry-red nails.

"Yeah," she says, "but it's nice how you're looking out for Darlene. Kinda wish my sister had been more like that, you know?"

Cindy gets up, wanders over to the washroom, and leaves me at the bar alone, feeling eight hundred times shittier than I did when I came in.

Things are pretty silent between me and Darlene as we drive over to Big Chip's trailer. She's still mad at me, and it's just as well because I'm lost in my own thoughts about Cindy and how maybe I am the world's biggest fuckhead for asking her to play nice with Big Chip just to save my somewhat undeserving sister.

We are pulling up to Big Chip's driveway when Darlene says, "You know what our bloody cousin Marni said to me while you were off in town?"

"How the hell should I know?" I snap. I take a right into the driveway a little too fast. The truck fishtails, and my hand slaps Darlene's as we both reach out to protect her stomach.

"Really, Charlie?" Darlene says and swats away my hand. "Marni said she doesn't know why Big Chip is taking me in in the first place, since it's clear I think I'm all that and he's just a rotten bag of Saltines. Said if it was her, she'd have told me to take my kid and shove it. Said I must be brain-dead if I think she's taking on any more work when the baby comes or lifting one goddamn finger to look after my brat. What a tool."

"So? She's always saying shit like that. And always looking out for number one."

"So maybe it's better I'm here with Chip. Not sure I want my Lexie hangin' out with the likes of Marni."

"And Big Chip is –"

"Can it, will ya? He's her dad, ain't he? Maybe I don't like it any more than you do, but there it is. They say some guys surprise you once they have a kid. Like it transforms them or whatever."

15

"And lightning might fly out my ass, Dar, but I'm not gonna plan my life around that possibility."

"Well, I'm willing to give Chip the benefit of the doubt. He said he'd try and do better. I think he's actually a bit excited about Lexie – in his way. Even started buying her toys and shit. You ever considered that the reason you hate Chip so much is you're just jealous how someone else has my attention?"

No. I'd never considered that, and right now I don't want to. I dig my fingernails into the steering wheel, try to keep my hands steady, and take a couple of slow, deep breaths as I look down the driveway. I feel heat rising in my cheeks and sweat starting to bead on my forehead because there, parked in front of the trailer, is Cindy Constantine's Mustang.

Darlene narrows her eyes and leans in close the way she does when she's trying to read my mind. "What the hell are you up to?" she says. I try to push the thoughts of Cindy straight out of my head.

"Nothin'," I mumble and give the truck a little gas. Whatever this is, I'm too deep in it to turn back now.

"You sore about me leaving?" Darlene asks. "I'm only gonna be four miles up the road. It's not like I'm moving to bloody Nunavut."

I pull up in front and think about Cindy there in the trailer – all the things she might be doing to help out my family. I realize I've been selling myself a line thinking I'm the only one in this town who knows the definition of hard work.

Darlene reaches over Lexie, who seems to be pressing the issue more by the second, and undoes her seatbelt. When Darlene sees Cindy's car, I can almost hear the gears in her brain start to squeal.

"Christ's bloody momma," she says and then is out of the truck quicker than she jumped off that fence yesterday.

Darlene marches up to the trailer door like a war-worn soldier who's got one more charge left before the final massacre.

16

Things start to close in on me, and there's zero chance I can keep my hands from shaking now as I sit in the truck and watch my treachery unfold. I think of my sister and what she is willing to sink herself into just so her little girl can have a daddy.

"And here's this bitch," I say to the silent interior of the truck, "hiding in the Chevy waiting for the whole situation to blow so she can get out her shovel, pile the shit back into the truck, and drive off like a thief."

I take one last look in the mirror and make my decision.

"Goddamn it," I mutter. "This is not how I want this to go down."

I leap from the truck and tear across the lawn after Darlene. I catch her arm just as she reaches the front window, and from the way I feel her body stiffen, I realize it's already too late.

I stand there in the fresh dark of the evening, holding onto my sister, and let the whole sorry scene sink in. There's Big Chip with his palms against the backrest of the couch, shaking himself from side to side. It doesn't take a genius to figure out what he's up to.

Darlene lets out half a scream, and Big Chip's head moves lazily upward. He looks past Darlene's approaching figure and lands his eyes straight on me. Darlene starts up the porch, but Big Chip doesn't flinch. He just holds my eyes.

It's not a pretty moment, standing here in the moist grass, looking into the cold eyes of a rattler and recognizing he's a fellow of my own species. I realize Big Chip and I have had the same thoughts, sent them down the same dark tunnel, and arrived here at the same destination.

Maybe Big Chip ain't so bad.

I hear someone approach behind me, but my brain is burning, and I don't turn around. A voice in my ear says, "She was here when I pulled in, so I figured I'd just stick around and watch the show." The small part of me that is still connected to reality realizes the voice belongs to Cindy.

A lot of things happen in succession. Dar whips open the screen door and enters the trailer. Inside, a woman jumps off the couch like a wet dog out of a river. Big Chip raises his middle finger toward the window and then turns to face the wave.

"You want a Mars bar, Charlie?" Cindy says to the back of my right ear.

I turn to face Cindy and the present wallops me like a whip.

"If it ain't you in there, Cindy, then who is it?"

"Who do you think?" Cindy says over her shoulder as she turns and walks toward her Mustang.

I take a better look around the dark yard and there, under the half-dead poplar, is a Dodge Ram half-ton. I've seen that truck too many times to second-guess who it belongs to. Our Marni.

Cindy gets in the Mustang and reaches over to pop the passenger door. "You wanna sit in the car with me till Darlene's ready to go?"

I'm not sure what else to do, so I get in the Mustang.

"Handle's busted," Cindy says as I try to ease back the seat. She points with her eyes to an open box of Mars bars in the centre console. "Have one if you want," she says. There is too much swimming in my throat to swallow anything more, so I just shake my head and take a look around the car's interior.

There's a sleeping bag and a pillow stretched out in the back seat, and I can feel Cindy's gaze on the side of my forehead.

I thought she would be doing okay enough in her line of work to have a place at least, so I'm surprised to see that sleeping bag lying there and telling me that everything is not how it seems.

"Things that bad for you, Cindy?" I say and then mentally kick myself for asking the obvious.

"Not as bad as they were."

Cindy lights a smoke and says, "I'm tired of screwing dudes for money. I've got to the point where I can't stand the feeling of their palms on my shoulders or that sad sound they all make just before they get off. I realized if I had to choose between a shitbox apartment and just one whole week that I didn't have to lay myself down for some vicious, lonely cock, I would choose B. You know?"

No. I don't know. It is becoming increasingly clear to me that I don't know shit.

Cindy peels back her Mars wrapper and fills her mouth with a hunk of soft chocolate and nougat. She leans back in the seat like we're at the drive-in and watches the scene flicker in the trailer window.

"Got three thousand dollars in my bank account," Cindy says when she stops chewing. "And in the evenings, Willie lets me take the leftover food from the bar. If I play my cards right, I won't have to screw anyone till winter – unless I want to."

It's a lot of information for me to be getting from someone I only talk to about twice a year. Still, I think about how me and Cindy have lived our whole lives together in this town and how, if we've had twenty or more conversations over that lifetime, that means that, apart from Darlene and Marni, Cindy is one of my closest friends.

"How long do you figure till she comes out?" Cindy asks, tipping her wrapper toward the trailer.

Darlene is standing by the window and looks to be chucking some of the smaller objects in the room at Big Chip's head. Over in the corner, Marni stands like a baseball catcher and whenever something reaches her, she just fires it on back. From the way Marni's laughing, it looks like she's having the time of her life.

"Another three minutes, maybe?" I say.

"Yeah, she's about done," Cindy says, jamming the last hunk of Mars bar into her mouth and squishing the wrapper into the ashtray on the dash.

"Listen, Cindy ... "

"I know, Charlie. I know. But you know what was worse? That you apologized. That made me feel like I actually wanted to help you."

"I was an asshole to even think – "

"Yep. You were. But I'm used to assholes, and you're a better asshole than most, I guess."

The trailer door squeals on its hinges, and Darlene comes chugging across the lawn.

"Time to go," says Cindy.

"Me and Dar didn't have supper yet," I say, "and I'm pretty sure our Marni won't be taking her share this evening. Do you want to come with?"

"This guilt talking, Charlie? I don't need your fuckin' sympathy."

"No, dipshit, it's about there being leftovers at my place and me not wanting to feed a good supper to the hogs. You want to eat another three Mars bars and puke in the ditch, be my guest."

Cindy smiles, reaches over the gearshift, and I almost leap out of my seat when she grabs my hand.

"Thanks, Charlie. It's a lot easier for me to deal with you when you're being a shit."

I've got no startle left to give when Darlene slams her open palm against the passenger window.

"Come the fuck on," Darlene hollers. "I can't fit behind the wheel of the Chev. Your goddamn girlfriend can follow us back to our place in her own car."

Darlene stalks back to the truck, and Cindy says, "How does she know I'm coming over?"

"She's the smart one."

I let go of Cindy's hand and roll my hips out of the seat.

Me and Darlene cruise down the side road in silence. The glow of the Mustang's headlights illuminates the side of Darlene's thick hair on the downhills. I can feel Darlene's deep hurt beating inside my own chest, and, though I long to put my arm across her shoulders, the whisper in my head tells me to leave it, to give her some room to breathe.

We're nearly home by the time Darlene leans her head against the headrest and says, "I can't blame her for taking what she wants, if someone's willing to give it."

"You mean Marni?"

"Who the fuck else, Charlie?"

Pretty much all of us, I think to myself and squint into the darkness so I don't miss our mailbox.

"Yeah," Darlene says and puts her hand up behind my headrest.

As we drive up to the farm, Darlene asks, "Did you feed the hogs before we left?"

I flick my eyes to the rearview to make sure Cindy is still following us. "Uh-huh."

I can feel Dar's eyes on me. She's got something else to say, but two can play at the silence game.

All is quiet in the hog barn as we pass it. I imagine the animals in there sleeping, asses still, fat bellies pressed together on the filthy straw as they snore, never dreaming of what might come next.

I pull up to the house, and as Cindy exits the Mustang, Darlene steadies herself against the Chevy's console and brings her lips close to my ear.

"Me and Lexie know you're thinking about kissing Cindy Constantine," she whispers.

Turns out I am.

The Many Coffees of Marissa

When things get too intense for Marissa, she buys herself a Cocoa Cluster Frappuccino, leans against the outside wall of her office building, and tells herself to breathe. When her heart rate returns to normal, she tips back her cup, reads whatever mashup of her name the baristas have written on its side, and for eight sweet minutes she closes her eyes and becomes that person.

MYLISSA

Mylissa is a ripped lioness with her jaw firmly clenched around the throat of corporate America. She had a great idea for the new lip balm campaign today, and at the strategy huddle she slapped that bad boy on the boardroom table and watched as the middle managers cowered in their minimalist, postmodern chairs.

(Before the huddle, Marissa bounced her idea off her cube-mate, Janelle. Janelle told her the idea was terrible but then presented it to the team at the meeting as her own. Marissa was too mortified to accuse her outright and simply said, "Great idea you had, Janelle," in a way she hoped sounded a bit sarcastic – but not overly so – because Jake, their manager, was listening. After the meeting, Marissa did not call her mother in Antigonish even though she wanted to. Instead, she sat with the phone in her hand and told herself to breathe.)

MARIKA

Marika is a cobra: precise and deadly. She smells subterfuge from fifty yards and strikes without remorse. After Janelle's betrayal, Marika stalked that duplicitous toad into the women's lavatory and devoured her whole.

(Later, when Janelle started bragging to Jeff from IT about "her" great idea, Marissa felt a panic attack coming on. She rushed to the washroom, and while she was in there doing her deep breathing, Janelle came in to apply more lipstick. Unable to contain herself, Marissa asked Janelle how she could stand herself, and Janelle told Marissa to keep her voice down and maybe get some counselling while she was at it. When she got back to her desk, Marissa did call her mother in Antigonish and told her a story that was mostly Marika's version of things. Her mother said, "That's my honey pie. Don't let the city girls get you down," and Marissa felt somewhat better.)

MERISHA

Merisha may look tame to the untrained eye, but she is directly descended from Actual Goddamn Amazons. She would sooner cut off her right breast than tolerate the chauvinist bullcrap of her manager, Jack, so when he suggested he take Merisha and Janelle out for coffee so they could "talk it out," Merisha called him on it, hard and fast. She got right up in Jack's face and asked him if he would approach a legitimate workplace dispute between two *male* colleges in the same "why don't you girls go get coffee and learn to play nice" sort of way? No? Didn't think so, Jackass.

(After Janelle refused to go to the coffee shop, Jack suggested he and Marissa go alone. While he sipped his half-caf soy latte, Jack let his hand linger on Marissa's forearm in a way she felt was too familiar and said that "a little bird told him" Marissa might be having some personal issues that were spilling over into her work life. After, Jack told Marissa he thought she looked "really svelte" in her new skirt. When it was time

to go back up to the office, Marissa told Jack to go on ahead and stayed back in the coffee shop to "get one to go." When she called her mother in Antigonish from the coffee shop's washroom and told her how things went down between Merisha and Jack, Marissa's mother said, "That ought to give that character a thing or two to chew on," but this time it did not make Marissa feel much better. Then Marissa's mother casually mentioned the weekend Lady Leaders course that their old neighbour Darla was teaching at Dalhousie and wondered aloud how long it would take Marissa to drive there from her apartment on a Saturday when there was no traffic.)

ALISSA

Alissa is a tiny piece of jalapeno who hides in your spicy chorizo breakfast sandwich. If you bite into her, she will set your whole damn world on fire. When Alissa was on her way back to the elevators, she noticed Jack standing at the security desk trying to throw his weight around with Venka, the agent on duty. Alissa, never one to let a sister down, marched right up to the desk, and together, she and Venka proceeded to roast Jack like the lightweight marshmallow he was.

(Marissa, unsure of what to do about bearing witness to the escalating situation between Jack and Venka, hovered uncomfortably in the general vicinity of the security desk and watched as Jack demanded to know who the hell Venka thought she was. Jack then informed Venka she was just some tattooed dumb-ass in a fake cop uniform, and he was goddamned if she was going to dictate where the manager of marketing went in his own place of work. Venka stood up from her chair and told Jack he had exactly five fucking seconds to apologize, and when he didn't, Venka reached over, laid her palms flat on his pectorals, and told him to back the hell up. Jack turned and stomped off toward the elevators. Marissa hung back just long enough to lean into Venka's ear and whisper, "Venka, I have never once admired a human being more than I do you right now.")

MARYSA

Marysa is a secret agent of the Republic of Whoop-ass and she's trained to maim. If you cross her, she'll take you down like 1970s wallpaper. Jack thought his troubles were over once he fled the security desk, but Marysa was just getting started. When she was leaving for the day, she backed her 2021 canary yellow Porsche 911 into Jack's entry-level BMW and burned rubber out of the parking lot. She lifted her clenched fist through the open sunroof and sped off into the hot afternoon, daring any of those corporate ass clowns to follow her.

(After Marissa came back up to her cubicle, Jack called her into his office. He said he was sorry she'd had to witness that ugliness at the security desk, especially since today was such an "emotional day" for her. While he said this, Jack pressed his knee against Marissa's thigh under the desk and slipped his fingers across the hem of her skirt. At that point, everything started to cave in around Marissa. She knew the panic attack of the century was coming on, so she backed out of Jack office, grabbed the keys to her mother's hand-me-down 1999 Corolla, and headed to the parking garage. In her desperation to flee the building, she miscalculated her exit from the parking space and accidentally hit the front fender of Jack car. She leapt from her car to assess the damage and stood like a tortured stone angel as the last drops of her reserve crashed to the concrete floor. Suddenly, Venka's voice echoed through the grey walls of the garage. "Just drive," Venka said. "I've already deleted the footage. I won't have a job here tomorrow anyway, so what the fuck. Don't let the bastards get you down."

Marissa stared into the security camera that was right next to her and mouthed "thank you" into the lens. As she left the parking garage, Marissa put her hand through the sunroof to wave at Venka in case she was still watching. That night, and for many nights after, Marissa did not call her mother. Eventually, her mother drove down from Antigonish. Marissa answered the door in her bathrobe and her mother said, "Tell me all about it, love, every last bit," but Marissa wasn't ready to talk yet, so she just stood there in the doorway and let her mother hold her.)

AIKO

Aiko is a modern-day Wonder Woman and she's ready to smash right through the glass ceiling. She heard the girl she replaced had some sort of nervous breakdown, but Aiko is not going to let herself meet the same fate. During her third week of work, Aiko noticed a note scrawled on the inside of the cardboard sleeve of her caramel no-foam macchiato.

If you want to survive this shark tank, please note the following:

1. *There is a toad lurking in the cubicle beside you. She will betray you.*
2. *Your manager has fast hands and a penchant for gaslighting. Take notes. There are human rights laws in this country that are about to blow his friggin' mind.*
3. *Caffeine is a terrible cure for anxiety.*
4. *Don't ever lie to your mother. She can see right through you.*
5. *If you require backup, Dalhousie's Certificate in Women's Leadership is taught by a kickass woman named Darla. Registration for the next session closes in eight weeks.*
6. *Marissa, the somewhat aggressive new barista at the coffee shop, is your ally. She and her roommate, Venka are saving up to enroll in the course at Dal. Tip her well and often.*
7. *Don't let the bastards get you down.*

Fingered

Manuela has received no invitation to her sister, Sofia's, funeral. Yet here she is.

She sweeps past Fidel, who sputters like an unwatched pot, and reaches the point where the grass ends and her sister begins. Fidel is quick. He presses his smooth nails into Manuela's arm and commands her, in a low roar, to leave.

She refuses.

Fidel is unaware that restraining orders terminate upon death and that his authority expired two days ago, along with Sofia. Manuela takes a drag on her Esplendido and whispers to Fidel, on the exhale, that his luck has finally run out. She lets the smoke hang between them and slides her fingers over the smooth something she keeps in her pocket. She considers the deep caves of Fidel's ignorance.

Fidel doesn't know Manuela lives in an apartment on the Danforth with a balcony that hovers, like a restless hornet, fifty meters above the edge of his own backyard.

Fidel doesn't know Manuela, her rocking chair, and her binoculars are the reason he associates summer evenings with the smell of Esplendido.

He must remember the stairwell. His voice was the loudest of any as he had bellowed, through bloodied lips, that Sophia no longer had a sister, that any woman claiming to be that sister would be arrested on sight if she ever returned to his matrimonial home. He must remember the police and Sophia's quiet weeping beneath the stairs. That much he knows.

But Fidel doesn't know Manuela can see through words and walls and people; that when Sophia had begged her to stay away, Manuela had known she didn't mean it. When the judge had proclaimed Manuela a menace, she had seen Fidel's dollars laughing behind those judicial eyes.

Fidel doesn't know the fraying curtains of his bedroom window have been insufficient to conceal his secrets. That tears, although silent, can disturb the ears of sisters who know how to listen. That whole stories can be told through a set of binoculars by the way a sister rocks herself on her porch swing at the end of the day.

Fidel doesn't know that when Sofia got her own set of binoculars, the sisters were content to just stare at each other's bruises – Sofia's obvious, Manuela's less so – because by then there was nothing left to say. That they watched and rocked and waited.

Fidel doesn't know that when Sofia lost her finger in the lawnmower accident, she did eventually find it.

Fidel doesn't know it was wedged between the rosebush and the shed.

Fidel doesn't know that after a three-hour search, Sofia crossed to the middle of the yard and held the finger up against the dangling rays of the evening sun so Manuela could see it through her binoculars.

Fidel doesn't know that the next day Manuela received a package, the contents of which she carefully mummified in the dry heat of her kitchen window and then carried for forty-four years in her coat pocket.

Fidel doesn't know what is descending now, from Manuela's unclenched fist, into the dry earth.

But he will in a moment.

The gentle thing lands like a songbird atop Sofia's casket.

Fidel's eyes shift from fog to darkness as the finger comes into focus.

Manuela is glad she has come to the funeral, despite no invitation, despite everything. It means she is here to see, with her naked eyes, what Fidel now knows.

That there were parts of herself that Sofia had managed to save.

Return of the Waxwing

When Ruth hits the yard, she's still in her housecoat. She is too damn old to dress up for anything, even a murder. Ruth smashes the settings on the bug zapper to high as she descends the porch steps. She takes her axe in one hand and a syringe full of herbicide in the other. Tonight, Leon Hishon's poplar is going down.

The tree has grown eight feet in the three years since Hishon arrived from England to "go rogue" in Slave Lake. For the past three weeks, Ruth has watched with displeasure as that barky bastard drops its yellow leaves across her birdbath. The bath's water has grown so foul that even the fat wrens have started to think twice about a dip. Ruth hasn't seen a waxwing in weeks, and she knows exactly why. The waxwing is a fine bird. Elegant. Classy-like. Not liable to dip his toe into some gangly poplar's filthy leavings.

Hishon has it coming. Ruth has knocked eight times in as many days, but the old loon won't darken his door. The ruffle of the curtain in his upstairs window tells Ruth all she needs to know about the strength of Hishon's spine. Afraid to face her. Like they all are. Goddamn men.

Last summer, Ruth's ex-husband, Reggie, had told her she was "terminally friggin' aggressive" right before he had tried to drive off with most of their casino winnings and her budgie, Cecile.

When the cop filled out the incident report that had followed, he wrote that Ruth *displayed poor self-control during the dispute.* Screw the both of them. Ruth was not put on this earth to please people.

Ruth holds the axe aloft as she trudges across the freshly shorn grass. There is no need to be coy about this killing. Most of the neighbourhood, herself and Hishon included, are in their seventies and more likely to be snoring into their pillowcases than keeping watch over their yards.

Ruth hikes up her flannel nightshirt and eases her veined legs over Hishon's fence. Ruth is not skinny, but she is light on her feet when she needs to be.

Ruth's slippers slap the moist earth beside the poplar's roots. She leans back, takes her stance, and squints into the darkness.

A shriek springs forth from the poplar's trunk. Ruth startles, belts out a war cry, and drives her axe blindly into the wood. When given a choice between anger and any other emotion, Ruth invariably chooses anger.

"Step one is to understand that you are not powerless against your rage," says the tree, and Ruth jumps backward. "Picture a stop sign on the road ahead. Heed it, Ruth. Give your thoughts permission to overtake your impulses."

The idea of a talking tree is asinine, but reason has become a tiny matchstick in the inferno of Ruth's mind.

"You think I'm gonna take advice from some deciduous smart-ass, you've got another thing coming," Ruth bellows. She cocks the syringe, but her stab is interrupted by Leon Hishon slinking out from behind the tree.

"But will you take advice from a born philosopher and soon-to-be-certified life coach?" he asks in a voice more placid than one would expect from a man who has just narrowly escaped a grisly maiming.

Ruth appraises Hishon and is surprised by his attire. The few times she has seen him skulking about the neighbourhood, Hishon has been dressed in a faded linen shirt and some ridiculous

31

bow tie, but tonight, a vintage Rolling Stones tee is stretched across his skeletal chest.

"Life coach?" says Ruth. "Thought you were supposed to be some kind of professor."

"Never made tenure, I'm afraid. Not much of a pension. Multiple income streams and all that, I thought I'd try out this new 'coaching' craze that appears to have set the millennials ablaze."

Ruth eyes the pale husk of a human hunched before her and snorts. "Life coach my ass, Hishon. Who the hell are *you* gonna give life advice to? Some of your old pals down at the vampire's supper club?"

Despite her expectations, Hishon seems delighted by Ruth's words. He leans toward her and says, "We are both creatures of the night, it seems."

"Don't go shoving me in *your* slop-hole, Hishon. I'm way outta your league." Ruth wonders why she is even still talking to this washout.

"You're a huge person, Ruth," Hishon whispers. "I have always admired that about you."

"Gonna make wisecracks about my weight now, are you?" Ruth fumes. "I've been alive longer than the goddamn Prime Minister. I want a piece of pie, I'm gonna have it. With ice cream if I feel like it."

"Of course, Ruth. Whyever wouldn't you?" Hishon says. "You are a woman who does precisely what she likes to, that much I know."

Ruth pulls her housecoat tight around her body, suddenly wary of how much Hishon claims to know. "You been spying on me, you old creep?"

"Not *spying*, per se," Hishon replies. "I'm sure you'll agree that being neighbours, our relative proximity means we are often obligate bedfellows in each other's mundanities. I'll bet you a thin Canadian dime you could name a few of my own quirks and quarks."

Hishon pulls a dime from his pocket, flips it in the air, and removes it from behind Ruth's ear. Ruth takes an abrupt step backward and says, "Like how you never bother to cut back your lousy poplar?"

"Quite," says Hishon. "Say nothing of our mutual appreciation of the waxwings who dwelt there. They have gone now, but did you see their nest in the branch overhanging your garden?" As Hishon recalls the birds, his voice reminds Ruth of a hypnotist in Vegas who once encouraged her to do a chicken dance on the casino's stage. "I couldn't bear to trim it," Hishon continues, "despite its obvious assault on your birdbath. Perhaps the pair will return next spring."

Ruth coughs and slips the herbicide syringe into her housecoat pocket as Hishon walks to the tree and rips the axe from its trunk with surprising strength.

"In truth," Hishon continues, "I *did* stand a little closer to the window than was necessary when you finally chased off that git Reginald. First time I have seen a suitcase so successfully dropkicked through a windshield, by the way. I said to myself, 'Leon, if only *you* could live your *own* life so viscerally.' I don't mind telling you, Ruth. You were part of the reason I decided to become a life coach. I see you as sort of a … how should I say it?"

"Queen among vermin?" Ruth offers as her eyes slide back to Hishon's T-shirt and the smooth, moist lines of the Rolling Stone's tongue graphic.

"Precisely," Hishon says, following Ruth's gaze. "Best band of our generation, eh Ruth? 'As Tears Go By' seems a 3:00 a.m. favourite for both of us." Hishon pauses to consider how the axe blade shimmers in the moonlight. "Do you miss him terribly? Is that why the rage?"

Ruth looks past Hishon and into the dark yard. Of course she misses him. Reggie hadn't been much, but at least he'd been another warm body beside her on the porch. Hishon takes a step toward her. "There is no shame in it, Ruth. Most of us only miss the ones who don't deserve us."

"Anyone ever miss you, Hishon?" Ruth asks and instantly regrets it. Ruth's nerves are buzzing from Hishon's creeping proximity, and she wishes she had not given him an excuse to dive deeper into their conversation.

"Barely," says Hishon as he drops the axe and glides his pale fingers through his dishevelled hair. "Too strange a bird for most, I'm afraid. Wound too tightly to reveal myself for fear I'd say something gauche. Despite what the novelists tell you, nobody ever falls in love with a professor. Not for very long, anyway."

"That's a hell of a mouthful for a man who claims to be dead wood," Ruth says. "Sounds like you're feeding yourself a lot of hocus pocus."

"It's kind of you to say, Ruth. I suppose that's what the life coach business is about. 'Physician, heal thyself' and all that bollocks." Hishon presses his fingers together as if in prayer. "Say, Ruth, won't you let me help you slay that rage of yours? I'll never get anywhere if I can't practice my skills on real people, and I do love a challenge."

"I don't go in for that nonsense."

"Oh, please, Ruth?" Hishon whispers through his fingers. "Just for a wee moment?"

Hishon opens his hands and offers Ruth the dime. "Take it," Hishon says. "I implore you."

Confused, Ruth removes the dime from Hishon's hand.

"Quick now," Hishon says, "give it back to me."

"Why the hell should I – "

"Do play along, Ruth. Go on. Give it here."

Ruth presses the dime back into Hishon's palm with significantly more pressure than is necessary. Hishon snaps his fingers closed. "Perfect!" he says. "My first paying client!" Hishon tucks the dime in his pocket, waves his hands as if conjuring a low-grade spell, and recommences speaking in his hypnotic voice. "Okay," Hishon says. "Close your eyes, Ruth. Can you do that for me?" Despite herself, Ruth complies. "Now, imagine your special place. Somewhere you feel at peace with the universe."

Ruth thinks of Vegas and the big pool in front of the Bellagio, the way the water glows pink right before the fountains shoot their spray. She opens her eyes a crack to see Hishon pacing a circle around her, twisting his body and gracefully raising his arms. When she recloses her eyes, Ruth sees a vision of the waxwing, the shimmer of his neck feathers as he splashes in the water. She feels a warmth descending toward her, and then, for an electric second, Hishon's bony fingers land atop her forearm.

"Tell me what you see, Ruth," he says.

A Ferris wheel of feelings clatters through Ruth's body: excitement, fear, and then, inevitably, rage.

Ruth slaps Hishon's hand and stomps back toward the tree. "It's none of your damn business what I see, and keep your claws to yourself," she barks over her shoulder.

Hishon is quick to retreat. "I'm sorry, Ruth," he calls, his expression downcast. "I should never have agreed to guide you, not when I knew I was so inappropriately conflicted."

"What the hell are you on about now?" Ruth says as she stops and turns back to Hishon. "Why can't you just speak plain?"

Hishon mumbles his words into the grass, so low Ruth can barely hear them. "That's how it always goes with me," he says. "Too bloody enthusiastic, aren't I? And next thing you know, I've made a mess of everything."

Ruth doesn't like the look of defeat that comes over Hishon's face. Maybe he'd been on to something there. God knows Ruth would like to feel more peaceful. But that's the problem with men; first sign of trouble, they lose their goddamn nerve.

"Cry me a river, Hishon," Ruth says. "One unlucky hand and you're outta the game, is that it? You're the crappiest life coach ever. I'll tell you why you spend your nights sneaking around your own backyard like some kinda pervert. Because you're limp-leafed, Hishon. Just like your sloppy-ass poplar."

"But I've compromised you, Ruth," Hishon says.

"Blow it out your pie hole, Leon. It's me who decides when

I'm compromised, and I'll tell you, it's gonna take a lot more than *your* fluttering fingertips to compromise Ruth Sowery. Get back on the horse." Ruth closes her eyes. "Hit me up, and stop being such a bellyaching flake."

"Ruth," Hishon whispers, "you are simply peerless."

Ruth listens to the sound of Hishon's furtive footsteps as they approach her, wills him forward with her furious mind. "Come on," she says. "Stop screwing around."

"Alright, Ruth," Hishon says. "This time, I promise not to disappoint you. Can you take a slow, deep breath?"

Ruth breathes richly of the cool night air.

"We are going to do a self-truth exercise," Hishon murmurs, the hypnotic quality of his voice gathering steam. "When I ask you a question, I don't want you to hesitate. I want you to say the first thing that comes to your mind. Can you do that?"

Hishon's words surround Ruth like fresh-fallen dew. "I guess," she says.

"I want you to picture yourself walking on the sidewalk outside your house. It's early, and the sun is just starting to crest the distant horizon. Are you there with me, Ruth?"

"Uh-huh."

"Let all that moist morning concrete surround you like a simmering womb."

"Sure."

"Good. Now I'm going to tell you something. It's Thursday. What does that mean to you, Ruth?"

"Garbage day."

"Precisely. And tell me, Ruth, what do you see in front of you?"

"The big black bins."

"Perfect. Now here comes the question, Ruth. Are you ready?"

"Yeah."

"Was it you, Ruth, who painted GO BACK TO OXFORD, ASS CLOWN, on my rubbish bin?

"Yeah."

Ruth's eyes snap open.

The bastard.

Hishon lets loose another unexpected shriek. "Got you good, Ruth!" he cries.

As Ruth runs her angry eyes over Hishon's face, it occurs to her she has never, before this moment, inspired such happiness in another human being.

The Ferris wheel spins again in Ruth's chest: anger, excitement, anger, and then, unexpectedly, mirth.

Ruth springs forward, wraps her fist around Hishon's diminutive wrist, and says, "Leon, you want to come back to my porch, watch the bugs crackle, and listen to 'Honky Tonk Woman'?"

Hishon's eyes alight, and he says, "That sounds like an absolute dream, Ruth, but ... "

Here it comes, thinks Ruth as she watches Hishon's face crumble. *You finally put your toe in, and they can't screw you over quick enough.*

"But what?" demands Ruth, though she can barely stand to hear the answer. Hishon's expression is tortured as he says, "It would just be so ... inappropriate."

The beast in Ruth rises again. "There's nothing friggin' inappropriate about – "

"Don't you see?" Hishon says. "We have already established a life coach–client relationship." Hishon pulls the dime from his pocket and places it in his open palm.

Ruth looks back across the lawn, past the faint outline of her birdbath, and on to the glow of the bug zapper where it lies in wait on her porch. She hears a snap, then a sizzle, and she makes her decision.

Ruth snatches the dime from Hishon's hand and flips it up toward the stars. When the dime falls, she catches it atop her glistening tongue, and, as Hishon beholds her with his mouth agape, she swallows the dime down.

Ruth's slippers smack against her calloused heels in staccato as she turns and darts toward the fence. Ruth doesn't need to turn around to know that Hishon is following her. She can feel him swooping in, his arms raised like yellow-grey wings.

Elegant. Classy-like. The finest bird Ruth has ever seen.

Class Party

Keri-Ann was wearing her mama's yellow dress, the one from some party before the bad-luck days.

She slid her socks across the kitchen tiles, quiet as cotton snakes. She pressed past the pipes and bottles scattered on the counter and eased open the cupboard. Way at the back, in the dark where she almost couldn't see it, was the last clean cup.

Keri-Ann turned the tap on low, filled the cup from the gentle trickle, and drank the water down in slow gulps. She wouldn't wake the bear.

There were no more crackers; she didn't bother looking. She'd wait till second period and sneak a granola from the box in Mrs. Harriet's drawer.

Mama wasn't much for shopping anymore.

Keri-Ann pulled up on the closet door so it wouldn't scrape the floor as she opened it. There was a mirror on its inside surface, and Mama's reflection swung into view. Mama's face looked sweet and peaceful as she slept on the living room floor, the way Keri-Ann remembered it from the good-luck days. Mama always looked more familiar when she wasn't awake.

But Keri-Ann didn't have time for sore thoughts. The school bus was on its way. She got busy digging in the closet, and she didn't hear Nana sneak up behind her.

"Where you goin' out to, looking like that?" said Nana.

Nana didn't know it was Halloween and the other kids would be wearing costumes their mamas sewed up because those mamas weren't out drinking like Keri-Ann's was. Nana didn't know much of anything anymore. Her brain had gone mush from too much living.

But Keri-Ann knew how to make a plan. She slipped on some canary gloves from winter, smashed her feet into last year's duck boots, and she was done. She had become The Sun, and her rays shot straight out of the front of her dress.

With hot hands and hurt feet, she ran out of the house before Nana could make a fuss.

The school bus came screaming down the side road, and the doors smashed open. Keri-Ann hopped up the three big steps, and, for the first time that year, she felt warm in her chest. She knew she looked perfect and good times were coming.

Shawn Kelvin, his new horns poking straight out from his forehead, hollered from the back:

"Hey, yo-yo, you a friggin' banana or what?"

Titter, choke, cough.

Keri-Ann didn't care. She stood up on the front seat of the bus and stared backward at all those demons and kittens. She moved her hands like two slithering rattlers, and the crazy asses stared and laughed. But Keri-Ann knew folks who looked directly at the sun would go blind, so soon they wouldn't be able to see her. She stayed there, shaking – all the eyes eventually looked past her, and before long, she was the only one who knew she was on fire.

Female Jockeys

On Christmas Eve, 1934, I was sipping soda at the Buchanan on 97th Street when a girl came over and scrambled my evening like a bowl full of eggs. She slid onto the seat beside me, and the ring she was wearing caught itself on the edge of my blouse. I looked down at the gentle curve of the girl's wrist, the way she ran her fingers across my sleeve to free the jewel, and I thought I might die. She drew her thumb across the green gem that was set in her band and flashed her eyes up to mine. "It's a fake, but a good one," she said. She gave me a wink like we were old pals and embers flared inside my cheeks. "What's a girl got to do to get a drink around here?"

The girl's lips were two inches from my face, and a hot thought ripped through me before I wrestled it back underground. I was not a quick or snappy sort of dame, but I was desperate to keep the girl's attention, so I took a chance and said, "Have a purse full of money or the eye of a fella?"

The girl's laughter fell over us like a warm drizzle. She leaned back on her elbow to appraise me, and I felt the edges of my collar squeeze against my neck. She looked down at my meaty hands, their nails bitten to the quick, and made her judgement. "That ain't what life's got planned for a couple of gals like us."

My eyes bounced over to old Alma, who was sitting down at

the end of the bar. I took a long breath and willed her to stay put, but I knew in my heart what was coming.

My mind drifted back to earlier that afternoon. I had been half-way through my seventh cigarette when Alma had announced we were going Christmas shopping. I had figured we were off to the dry goods store on the corner, but apart from a quick stop for Lucky Strikes, we had beaten a straight path to the back door of the Buchanan.

Alma had looked over her shoulder, eased open the door, and said, "We'll get all our gifts here this year, Rosie." My heart had sunk when she had said it because being in public with Alma was a special kind of hell. "We should be spending our money on gifts for the family, Rosie, but since they're all dead to us, we'll spend it on bourbon instead. One shot for each one of the goddamn bastards, down the hatch."

Alma had chuckled and disappeared through the door. I had stood outside and braced myself for a doozy of an evening. When Alma got a hold of her bourbon, she became the world's most enthusiastic charlatan. I knew she would take all of the poor saps at the Buchanan halfway to China before they had even realized they were out the front door.

I'd badly wanted to skip the whole situation, but there were two reasons I hadn't. The first being that despite hating her, I loved Alma. The second being that she was my mother, and even though I was twenty-six, I couldn't shake the feeling that I was obliged to do what she said.

So, I sat at the bar of the Buchanan, drinking soda, smoking my sixteenth Lucky Strike, and steeling myself for the inevitable. You wouldn't catch me swimming in bourbon and making an ass of myself downtown.

Alma slapped her coins down and called over Slim Bobby. "First one's for Bert," she said. Slim grabbed the bourbon without missing a beat, and I realized this wasn't the first time Alma had done her Christmas shopping at the Buchanan.

Bert was Alma's pa, who, despite his own hot temper and fast hands, had expected better things from his daughter than she had ultimately delivered.

Alma belted back her bourbon in one hard swallow and slammed her cup on the bar. "Worst father I never had," she said. Alma looked up, saw I was talking to the girl, and stood tall like a squirrel who'd seen a nut. She smoothed the ample bodice of her best house dress and coasted toward us. "Rosie, honey, ain't you gonna introduce me?" she said. The girl perked up for old Alma and offered her a hand. "Name's Phyllis, ma'am."

The way they shook hands was fishy. I saw Phyllis give Alma a little wink, and I wondered what the hell was going on. Slim slid a drink across the bar. "There you go, Philly, another Gin Rickey for my best girl," he said. Phyllis gave him a giggle, and I thought less of her for submitting to his oily charm. Alma knocked her empty glass against the bar. "Second one's for Freddie," she said.

Freddie was the slick mink who had once encouraged Alma to make a bad choice in the middle of a hayfield. The first lie Freddie had told Alma was that if she held still, it wouldn't be so bad. The second lie had been that he'd stay.

"Floppy-eared jackal, laughed me all the way to ruin," said Alma.

I touched the sides of my own oversized ears and thought about the sucker punch Freddie had landed nine months after he had gone.

Slim passed Alma her second bourbon and smiled. Alma raised her eyebrows, and they were thick as thieves. Phyllis sucked the lime from her Gin Rickey, and I snuck a better look at her. On a second pass, she lost some of her shine. Her pumps were a touch gauche, and she had a light fuzz over her top lip. That was all fine by me because the more that was wrong with Phyllis, the better the chance she would stay talking to me. It wasn't long before she caught me looking. "What do you say, Rosie," she purred, "am I just your size?"

I bit the inside of my lip and tried not to breathe. I knew what could happen to a girl who showed too much interest.

Alma got jittery from all the lack of attention and tipped her glass toward Phyllis. "Tell me, Phil, where's home?"

I knew what was coming next and I couldn't stand it. Alma and I lived in a couple of rooms above a five-and-dime, but that wasn't the story she was about to tell Phyllis. Whenever she started out asking someone where their home was, I knew she was about to do the horse-racing bit.

"I'm from Lethbridge originally, ma'am, what about you?"

Alma had her on the line then, and she and Phyllis were off to China.

"I'm a country girl, Phil. My pa owned near half of Shuswap out in the Rockies, and I was riding horses before I could walk," she said. I thought of the marginal operation north of Athabasca where Alma had spent her miserable childhood, and it was almost comical.

Phyllis forgot all about me at that point. That was how it always went. I would almost have a conversation with some nice-looking kitten, and then old Alma would come over and start laying down some story to scare her off.

"You see, Phil, my pa raced horses all the way from Whitehorse to Saskatoon, the finest fillies in the west. A lot of folks frown on a woman in the saddle, but not my pa. He let me ride those horses over God's great earth till I came home sore as sunshine. My brother never could swallow that I rode horses better than he could. If they'd let me race, I would have been a provincial champion."

I sipped my soda and wondered how she could stand herself. I knew who my people were, and I'd sell my own eyes if any forward-thinking British Columbian horse barons were among them. When Alma's pa had found out about her condition, he had told her he didn't have any daughter who whored herself out in a hayfield, so she had better just go ahead and get off his land and forget she ever lived there.

Alma paused her lying long enough to realize she was fresh out of bourbon. Slim poured the third shot and said, "This one's for Walter, if memory serves."

"On the money, Slim. Best brother Abel ever had."

Walter was Alma's big brother, who'd thought himself generous for offering to take Alma in. His only condition had been that she come without the baby. Given the terms of her tenancy, Alma had decided to skip town.

Alma had turned out to be a pretty awful mother, but one thing I could say for her was that she knew what was hers. It was easier to travel with a baby on the inside, so Alma had left the farm that very night, along with all the money in Walter's cash box.

I looked over at Phyllis, who was sipping her Gin Rickey and eating up Alma with her eyes. "I'd love to be able to ride a horse like that," she said. "I imagine it's a right thrill."

"Nothing better, Phil, than to be a female jockey."

I died inside when she said that, as if a female jockey was a genuine, actual thing. Phyllis was looking at Alma like she was pure churned butter and not just a drunk old hussy who lived above a five-and-dime with her lame-duck daughter.

As far as I saw it, I'd never had a chance. Alma had birthed me in the back room of an Edmonton tenement, and it wasn't long before we had found ourselves with no way to pay the rent. Alma being Alma, she gathered a few local floozies to alternate child-minding with working the streets. Most mornings of my childhood, I had woken up to some damp-haired beauty sleeping it off on our spare mattress.

"Last shot's for Marion, Slim."

Marion had been Alma's top floozy. It was her who gave me my first taste of hellfire, and I briefly considered ordering my own bourbon just for her. One night I had woken up to Marion's rum-soaked breath on my cheek and her saying, "Hey, Rosie, have you ever felt like kissing a woman?" Marion had caught my trembling lips in hers, and it was as close to Eden as I had ever been.

The next morning, Marion and Alma had blown the top off of everything, and as Marion was storming out the door, she had looked straight at me and announced to Alma, "Just so you know, sweetie, your girl Rosie is a bigger trapeze artist than you ever were."

When Marion had gone, Alma had looked at me with regret and said, "Rosie, those inclinations are pretty unsatisfactory. It's no way to live, believe me. The best thing you can do is to pretend to be some way else and find yourself a fella."

That was when I started the slow process of burying myself, and it probably went a long way to explaining why I couldn't talk to a girl without gnawing off my own hand.

I choked a little on my soda, and Phyllis gave me a quick look. I inspected my nails and realized that I had made a mess of things. Phyllis followed my gaze, saw the blood rising on the sides of my fingers, and lifted her pretty lips a titch. It reminded me of the way Marion had looked at me right before she'd closed the door.

Alma got impatient for the punchline of her story, so she started to run the home stretch. "I tell ya, Phil, it's a wondrous thing to climb on the back of a horse and just let it take you off to the other side of the sunset. It's the only time I've ever felt totally alive."

"But why did you stop, ma'am?"

Alma looked up, caught my eye in the reflection of the mirror behind the bar, and held it. "I got careless, Phil. Had a big fall off one of those animals and was too injured to get back in the saddle." A hot tear inched down Alma's cheek as she drained the last drops of bourbon from her glass. I might have felt sorry for her, had I not heard the story a hundred times and believed it less with each telling.

Phyllis and Slim turned toward me and from the way they were mugging, I knew they could see right through my skin and into the beating heart of the matter. Alma was crying in her bourbon, and you didn't have to look too far to see whose fault *that all* was.

Everyone got quiet and I knew they were expecting me to mop up the whole goddamn scene. My eyes burned, but you wouldn't catch me crying myself silly to a fuzzy-lipped honey and some two-bit soda jerk. I was so sore at Alma for the look she'd given me in the mirror that I did something I've never done before. I unseated the female jockey.

"You lie like you breathe, Alma. Your legs have been around a lot of things but never the back of a horse. If you ever fell off anything, it was the side of a bar." Phyllis laughed again, but this time the sound was more like cold hail.

Alma grabbed her purse and slipped off to the ladies' room while Phyllis downed the last of her Gin Rickey. "Why did you have to go and be so awful?" Phyllis said.

A shade was drawn over Phyllis' eyes, and I wondered why I had ever tried to fire her a snappy comment or let myself think about her pretty lips. I imagined Phyllis on Christmas morning, stuffing her mouth with sweets and forgetting all about the ham-fisted nobody she had met at the Buchanan. I thought about how that same tomorrow would find me sitting at the window above the five-and-dime, smoking my Lucky Strikes and listening to Alma say, "It's just another day."

"It's all lies, Phyllis. Can't you see? She's making fools of us."

Phyllis turned toward the bar and I saw in the mirror that her face had fallen. "It's only you who's the fool, Rosie. Nobody comes to the Buchanan on Christmas Eve because they're interested in the truth about things. Sometimes people just like to be sold a good story." Phyllis walked off without a backward glance and returned to her three companions at their table.

I was already feeling pretty rotten about everything, but Slim was next in line. He looked at me like I had just smothered a duckling and said, "You know what, Rosie? You should thank God that you have a ma like Alma. She frets about you, you know that? Says you're so sour she's not sure what you'll do when she dies and it's just you and your Lucky Strikes for company. She came in here yesterday and told me to look out for a young lavender she could possibly send your way."

I knew Slim was the worst kind of liar, so I didn't know what to believe. It didn't sit right with me, him talking about Alma dying and calling me a dyke as plain as day. "You don't know me from Adam, Slim Bobby."

"Don't know that I'd want to, Rosie."

Alma came back to the table, and she had fixed her face so you would never guess the fuss she'd made not ten minutes before. She looked at me with a familiar regret and said, "Nobody likes a stick in the mud, Rosie. Can't you pretend to be some way else? It's Christmas." My skull pounded and I wished she would make up her goddamn mind about how I was supposed to be. "Let yourself go a little, Rosie. Let folks see your sparkle."

I thought of myself sparkling; stroking my ring, sipping my Gin Rickey, and dancing home to swing the trapeze with a nice gal that I met at the Buchanan. I thought of old Alma, back in the saddle and finally riding free into the Rocky Mountain sunset. I hung there for a brief second and felt what it might be to live as someone different. The temptation to linger on that thought path was something awful, but you wouldn't catch me making myself into a lie.

"Ain't no sparkle, Alma, when a jewel is fake."

Alma turned around, leaned her elbows on the bar, and started to scan the room. I looked at the way the skin collected around her eyes, thought about what Slim had said about her dying, and felt a shiver.

Alma considered the desperate faces assembled in the Buchanan, and I realized that she hadn't finished her Christmas shopping. She was scanning the paltry offerings for a racehorse, one for her best girl to ride on through to the finish line. Then it was my turn to feel regret because I suddenly knew I'd never win that race. In the end, the only female jockey in the room was Alma.

"I wish I could ride a horse like you, Alma," I said, "but I'm afraid I'll never be able to shake the notion that we're just a pair of dirty old birds who can't fly farther than a couple of rooms above the five-and-dime." Alma reached over, grabbed my swollen fingers, and looked at me like she almost liked me.

"Could be," Alma said, "but that all sounds pretty unsatisfactory, don't it?"

The Poet of Blind River

It was 1999 when you came to me, Jimmy.

I was on a VIA train, eighty kilometres out from Pacific Central Station and caught up in a bit of a situation. The waves of that situation were coming on strong but instead of slipping beneath the surface of it, my mind lowered its anchor, and what it began to circle around was you.

I had locked myself inside the washroom of the train, had already been in there for twenty minutes, and soon enough some asshole would come and hammer on the door to find out what the hell was going on. But right then, at the moment I thought of you, I was still safe, still crouched on the lid of the toilet, a plank walker trying not to leap.

I rocked with the motion of the train and muttered the one thing I still remembered from rehab, the chant we were supposed to keep in our pocket for the end of the line, when we were just about to cave.

"I will not use for the next two minutes, and then I will decide."
Wait. Wait.
"I will not use for the next two minutes … "
And on it went until the asshole started banging.

I pressed my palms against my eyelids and the sudden rush of darkness made me think of a poem you had written back when we were seventeen – something about a bird's wing beating in the night sky – and it was a terrible poem, to be honest, all of them were, but still, the darkness made me think of it. The details eluded me, but I recalled the point of it had been the feeling you get when a whole lot of shit seems to be passing you by and you cannot catch a hold of any of it. I'd known the poem was really about me – they all were back then – and the thing we had always fought about: how I had never seemed to actually *feel* anything, at least not completely.

Should we really have been surprised that you never got anywhere with your poetry? I mean, how could you, with such a shitty muse? Maybe the real question should have been why a couple of northern kids like us ever thought we should try to express ourselves in a complex way? Probably we should have just stuck to underage drinking and fucking in the back of a Honda.

The rush of my inevitable screaming match with the asshole outside the bathroom was enough to grant me temporary reprieve from my craving, so I went back to my seat and had a look at the map in the seat pocket. The train was en route from Vancouver to Sudbury, and I was travelling on it to see about a job I had been offered in a marginal dogsled operation back home in Blind River.

I traced my finger over the names of the cities we would be stopping in, and when I got to Edmonton, I paused. I remembered how you'd moved out there after the breakup, and I started to wonder whether you might want to see me.

Part of me wanted to forget it because I'd accumulated a lot of scars since I'd last seen you. I had been a ripe fruit back when we were together, but I hadn't been kind to myself in the four years we had put between us. My rotten bits were starting to show, and I wanted to stay in your mind's eye as a force of the universe, the one who'd screeched out of the Food City parking lot on Huron Avenue and laughed while you chucked all your notebooks at the back of my Honda.

It felt good to think of you, Jimmy, like sucking on the hole of a missing tooth, and it went a long way to distracting me from my larger demons – the ones who told me to slip my fingers down into my pocket and caress the edges of the orange plastic container that was nestled there like a newborn kitten.

I looked up from the map and tried to watch the scenery as it whipped by the window. We were somewhere around North Bend, had just passed over the Fraser River. I tried to focus on the Rocky Mountains as they started to appear. I thought about how I was supposed to be "reconnecting with the beauty of the world," as my sister had advised. She had paid for my ticket, saying all the white peaks and blue sky would be just the thing to "snap me out of my funk."

You'll recall that was something I'd never been able to stand about my sister: her sickening optimism. Her solution for malignant depression? A nice hot bath. Life falling apart at the seams? Make a list. I realize it was kind of a screwed-up thing to dislike about someone, but back then I spent most of my time standing in a hailstorm, and all that sunshine was really starting to burn up my eyes.

That was the thing I always liked about us, Jimmy: the way we never felt guilty about how we acted. When we fought it was brutal, but in a way, it was also a thing of beauty. Holding it all in is killer sometimes, all that watching your words and trying not to act too feral, but that was never an issue with you and me. Once we got to howling, we would just keep at it until our throats were worn raw – but at the end of it all, we always came out feeling clean.

I remembered how when we were done scrapping, we would just lay down beside each other and wait for our breath to settle, how sometimes you would reach out your hand and we would just hang there while it all washed over us. I thought of how afterward we would take the Honda and park it out on the side road and you would grind yourself into me, like you were desperate to pin me down in that moment between pain and pleasure. I loved the way your voice got choppy right before you came, and how when you did you would cry out like you were almost surprised by it, like the sweetness just crept out of nowhere and bit you.

Remembering all of that made me think I shouldn't call you, that I'd done a pretty solid job of tearing out your insides before I'd left for Vancouver. The humane thing might be to just let you lie. But you know better than anyone how I've always been disinclined to leave well enough alone, so as the train lurched eastward toward the interior, I started to wonder how I could get your number.

I had given up looking at the mountains by then. It felt like they were mocking me, like they knew how goddamn beautiful they were and just wanted to throw it in my face. I thought about how their luminous peaks might disappear entirely if I just let myself take a few hits from my orange container. I knew from experience, though, that once I started thinking down that path, the slope got steep pretty quick, so I started to look around for someplace else to put my mind.

The lady beside me was rummaging through her purse, and when she pulled out a cellphone, I found my new focus. Not everyone had a cell back then, so I started asking her about how it worked. She was pretty okay with me at first, but after a while she got freaked out by my pressured inquiries. The thing was, I couldn't shut up because by that point that lady and her goddamn phone were the only things standing between myself and another trip to the washroom.

I asked her if I could use the phone to call up somebody I needed to reach in Blind River. She wasn't too keen, but my powers of negotiation were pretty rock-solid after three straight years of haunting emergency departments looking for Percocet scripts. Eventually, she just sighed and handed it over.

I couldn't quite recall your old number, but my fingers knew the pattern on the keypad from dialing it a hundred times a day back when I was seventeen. As it started to ring, I made a deal with the universe. I told it if the number was right, I would put the pills back in my suitcase until at least Jasper. I made a lot of decisions like that back then by just holding my breath and wait-

53

ing for the universe to decide if it was going to throw me a bone or just pull out the fucking rug.

Your mom answered on the second ring, and she spoke to me like she was punched up drunk to hear from me, like the breakup and all that ugliness after it had never happened, and I was just one of her old gal pals. I thought of her standing there in your old kitchen, winding that pink phone cord through her fingers while she shot the shit, and I wondered what it would be like to be her – to be that ordinary – for just one minute.

She launched into that story that always drove you buck wild, the one about how your creeper dad had been driving a streetcar through Toronto back in the 1970s. Your mom had been his last passenger at the end of the line, and she told me how, deep in the middle of that rainy night, old Barry had shut the streetcar's doors tight. He refused to let her off until she gave him her number. She hadn't liked the look of him – who could blame her? – so she just sat there and watched as the drops streaked down the windows for the better part of twenty minutes. Then desperation had gotten the better of her, and she had relented.

She loved that story more than anything, and even though I couldn't see her, I knew she was smiling like a cat on a sun-baked windowsill as she told it. I've always admired your mom's ability to weave a tender love story out of the fact that your dad basically held her hostage on public transit.

I'm not sure why I cut her more slack than my sister. Maybe I liked the fact that your mom paid the price for her romantic notions and got to ride that sweet delusion through twenty-five years of a shitty marriage and three out-of-control kids. There were a lot of things in my own life that might have been easier to stand if only I had her ability to ignore the parts of my story that didn't fit with the overall vision.

Right before we rang off, she gave me your new number and said, "Good luck, honey. I hope you manage to reach our Jimbo," and I almost choked up because at that point in my life, I was no longer used to such uncomplicated encouragement.

I didn't feel like having a Courtney Love moment right there in plain view of my seatmates, so I pushed past the phone lady and headed down to the luggage zone to pay my dues to the universe. The lady got up from her seat and started to chase me down the aisle, yelling, "Hey-hey-hey." I realized I'd forgotten to return the phone, so I thrust it backward, told her to fucking relax, and carried on down the aisle.

As I locked my little bitches up in my suitcase, I thought about how my life might have been different if I'd been able to get a more solid grip on things. How if I'd never broken my hand and discovered Percocet, we might have been able to skip the whole scene at Food City. Maybe you would never have written me that poem called "Go Fuck Yourself." Maybe instead we would have been living in some shit-box out on Michigan Avenue with a couple of kids, and I would be giving you grief for spending all your afternoons upside down and waist-deep in some broken engine while our kids screamed circles around my ankles and drove me crazy. I considered how everything had turned out, on my end anyway, and I decided that life might not have been so terrible.

When I got back to my seat, my seatmate was gone and so was all her stuff, so I was alone for the fourteen hours it took us to get to Jasper. Sleep eluded me. I sat there fidgeting and measuring the hours in two-minute intervals. I tried to break things up a little by looking out the window. There was nothing to see beyond all that night. I thought about the Rockies and how they were still out there, even though they were invisible. I thought of their ancient origins and my own impermanence, all that cliché shit people think about when they're near mountains, and as the train cut through the thick of the interior, I started to enjoy the feeling of being surrounded.

I got to thinking about that night we fell asleep naked in your basement after we'd finished screwing because we were still only sixteen and had that tiredness of little kids in us. I remembered how somewhere in the early morning, boozehound Barry had come to stand at the bottom of the steps, and you and I had pretended to still be sleeping while he hovered there and watched us like the creep he was. I guess we should have been scared, lying there exposed like that, but I think we weren't because we'd both known that together we could have kicked his ass if it had come down to it.

All of that nostalgia must have knocked me out cold because the next thing I knew we were pulling into Jasper station.

There was a payphone right on the platform. The skin on the back of my hand where I'd written your number started to burn, but when I disembarked the train, I blew right past that phone and cut a straight path to the washroom.

The thing was, when I got so close to calling you, I lost my nerve. The way we'd left things hadn't really seemed open to a reconciliation. I was afraid that all the bullshit that had happened to me in the interim might have left me too damaged to stand your ire.

I entered a stall, got up on the toilet lid, and closed my eyes, but the sweet thoughts wouldn't come. All I could think about was the Percocet and the moment when I'd put it back in my pocket before leaving the train. I tried to do my chant, but the minutes were suddenly too long, so I took out the bottle and tried to crack open the seal. I couldn't get the bastard undone, and as I started to bang the lid against the side of the stall, I realized what was happening: the universe was cackling.

I bolted from the stall and pretty well ripped the receiver off that platform payphone as I hammered in your number. I listened to the phone ring, and I dared the shit-for-brains universe to let you answer.

When I heard your voice, the words gummed up in my throat, and I just stood there like a dunce while I listened to your litany of hellos. It wasn't until you started screaming, "Who the fuck is this?" that I snapped back into gear and told you to just can it and get your ass over to meet me at Edmonton Station when the train rolls in at 7:30.

Even though we hadn't spoken in four years, we just sort of picked up right where we'd left off. You said you were just on your way to work, for fuck's sake, and did I ever think of giving a person some goddamn proper notice? I could hear a dull thumping in the background, and I knew you were whacking your palms against the sides of your thighs the way you had always done when you were pissed at me. Some old guy came up and started grabbing hold of my arm and yelling at me to get back on the train, so I told him to piss off, but you thought I was talking to you. You started to get fired up and I kept telling you, "Shut the fuck up and let me talk – just shut the fuck up and let me talk ... "

Then you told me to go fuck myself and it was just like old times.

Once we were rolling on the train again, I thought about your breakup poem and a couple of the lines came back to me: "You will bury me / but when I rise from my grave of shit / it will be middle finger first / pointing skyward / at you / my sweetheart." I thought of all the intricate drivel I'd listened to in west-coast coffee shops, and how none of it had been able to hold a candle to the raw honesty of "Go Fuck Yourself." Those lines had been the purest form of art, just a sloppy, burning hurt that oozed all over the page.

Even the sweet memory of your teenage rage could only hold me for so long, and I doubt even a minute passed before tiny bits of green pills started to drift across my mind. It occurred to me then that I might never be cured of my addiction because it would always be there waiting for me to claim it. Even if I left it for a day, a year, or even four, I would probably return to it eventually – that high seemed too sweet to give up forever. I pushed my thumb hard into the top of the bottle, but it held tight, and I decided to wait another two minutes, then another two, and so on and so on, until eventually, by some miracle, we reached Edmonton.

I'd already told myself you wouldn't be there. Why would you be? After the phone call, the Food City parking lot, after everything that had happened, and hadn't. But I still felt my heart quicken as I hopped off the train, so I made the universe one last deal: I told it to put you on that platform, and if it did, I would throw my stash in the garbage before I got back on the train.

But you weren't there.

I slipped out the side door of the station with the bottle rattling in my hand and marched out to the parking lot to find myself some privacy to get high. While I was crossing the pavement, I kept thinking about how it was going to mean three months of rehab down the shitter, but I didn't care. I just did not care, but I *did* care, just a little. That little bit was enough to make me look back at the station one last time, and there you were, sitting behind the wheel of your work van, staring your angry lightning rods at the arrivals door.

You big dumb fuck, there you were.

The Percocets seemed to scream bloody murder as they ricocheted on the inside of trash can. I walked around to the passenger side and just stood there. I waited for you to notice me, and as I did, something started warming me up from the inside.

I thought about how you had come to the station even though you were mad at me, how in some way you must still be on my side, and for that one minute as I stood there and looked at you, I knew what it might feel like to be ordinary, to have things in life I could depend on.

You looked like a top-grade asshole as you scowled through your windshield at the exiting passengers, but I could see that kid behind your eyes, the one who had tried to write poems, the one who had tried to solve things, the one who had tried to find small pockets of happiness in this rotted-out world.

As the stream of people thinned from the arrivals door, I watched as disappointment started to creep around the edges of your eyes. That was when I started to bang on the hood of your van because more than anything at that moment, I wanted you to see me.

I don't think I even said hello before I stuck my tongue down your throat, and you kissed me back hard because I think we both knew that train would be leaving in forty-five minutes, and this was the last stop for us, that after the universe paused for those brief moments, we would permanently travel in different directions and never crash into each other again.

It's been four years since they decided to rip up Queen Street, and as I stare down at the mess they've made beneath my apartment window, it occurs to me that they will never completely fix it. There is a construction guy pacing the ruptured sidewalk below; he screams obscenities into his cellphone and waves his tattooed arms through the steam of the afternoon. In a different life, I would have leaned across my sill and shouted down an invitation. But today, I think I'll skip it.

I've been holding myself closer these days. I've been taking better care. Even my sister has started to come back around to a cautious hope that the seasons, for me, might be finally changing. So, instead of plunging down there into the heat and mess of the day, I will sit up here at my third-hand desk and think about all the shit that seems to have passed me by.

I picture you as you might look at this precise moment, perched atop some oil rig in the middle of a sand swamp. You've probably gotten paunchy from too many hours spent in a Fort Mac sports bar, swigging your beers and yelling your insults at a shiny big screen. I imagine your eyes grown tired, and how your face must hang loose now, like mine. Forty-six years, Jimmy. Forty-six years of living on the edge of things.

Does that afternoon you met me at Edmonton station ever cross your mind? As you try to ignore that last whiskey in the mini-bar and spread yourself wide atop that pale-patterned comforter, do you ever look over to the identical bed beside you? Do you wonder what it would be like if that bed was occupied? If the universe had just thrown me down beside you and let me stay?

I heard your mom moved in with your sister a few years ago, after your dad's accident. So, even if my fingers still remembered your old number, that tap dance over the digits would only deliver me to somebody else's kitchen or the sound of a disconnected line.

And I'm proud to tell you, Jimmy, that I have finally learned a thing or two about leaving things be, so I will not even try, this time, to track you down.

But there are some things I think the universe wants you to know.

It wants you to know that I held on to those moments we stole together in the summer of '99, stored them inside myself for years afterwards, through all sorts of terrible shit you do not ever need to consider.

It wants you to know those brief moments of life in the train station parking lot gave me hope where I might otherwise have had none, and that sometimes, even the smallest shreds of hope can be braided together to form a rescue line.

It wants you to know that as all those crates and tools smashed down around us in the back of your work van, I felt the molecules of my brain start to buzz, and finally, as I drove you inside of me, that I felt every inch of you.

For two sweet minutes.

Completely.

Lions in the Clouds

"No pulse," Dorothy says. "Not surprised. She's already cool."

Lynn's eyes track the trail of red mist that has settled onto the hard-packed snow as Dorothy points her chin in the direction of the truck. Lynn dons her glasses to consider the stained tailgate. Their sister Flora is a mess below them, coated in a thick layer of blood.

"Looks like she cracked her head on the way down," Dorothy continues. "The bumper, I figure."

"Probably right," Lynn says. "Coffee cup's spilt there beside the back tire. You flip her over yourself?"

"Yup. Had to be sure."

Lynn nods as the bile creeps up the back of her throat. Dorothy has always been the hardest sister of the three. The farm would fail in a second without her, and Lynn knows it. "A better man than most men" is what they say about Dorothy in town.

"Steady now," Lynn tells herself. The last thing they need right now is for her to go squirrelly.

Despite her reluctance to fully consider the reality below her, Lynn feels strange about towering over Flora. She kneels beside her sister's body, and, to avoid looking directly at her ruined face, runs her fingers across the tightly knitted rows of Flora's bright pink toque.

"Think we should call the medics?" Lynn says.

"Nah," says Dorothy, who has always been practical. "Better to wait a while and let her stiffen up some, so they don't get any ideas. Life she's lived, she don't need to go out with them jumping all over her."

Lynn eases a few of the toque's fibres free from the icy ground beneath Flora's scalp. Frost pellets crackle under Dorothy's boot treads as she shifts her weight forward to get a better look.

Dorothy pats the front pocket of her work shirt, fishes out a smoke, and flicks it toward the toque.

"Remember where Mother got the wool?" says Dorothy.

"Discount bin at Lizanne's," says Lynn.

"Pure merino for two cents a yard and no sense griping about the colour," they say in unison.

Lynn snorts, as she often seems to in sombre moments. She remembers how Mother had knitted all three of them the matching toques back in '57 and how Father had told her no person in their right mind would wear a hat that pink. "Acrylic yarn won't stand up against a Saskatchewan winter," Mother had replied. "And we all have to eat."

Dorothy lights her smoke and considers the budding embers of the horizon.

"Musta come out to watch the sunrise," she says and looks down the slope of the driveway that leads to the road. "She was always funny like that."

"Figure her ticker?"

"It'll be the same for all of us, I guess. Family of bad hearts."

Lynn thinks of their parents, both thirty years cold in their graves of heart attacks, and probably happier for it. She thinks of the three empty plots that wait beside them and how they will soon have to dig out the first of them.

Dorothy presses the toe of her boot against Flora's arm to test the waters. The arm rolls freely against the slick ground.

Not ready yet.

The bile recommences its ascent of Lynn's throat, and she feels a fist start to tighten in her chest. She looks out across the bean field to where the clouds hang low atop the fallow stocks, grey as gunmetal.

Dorothy clicks her lighter and takes a pull on her smoke. "Maybe saw a lion in one of them storm clouds, and it scared the living shit out of her."

Lynn laughs, though she does not think the joke is funny.

Flora had always been the type of person to see things that others didn't. Running off across the bean fields to the north woods when she should have been working, writing all sorts of nonsense in her spiral notebooks, and seeing a whole jungle of animals winking at her from the winter sky when all the rest of the family could see was a blizzard coming on.

"Not surprised she went first," Lynn says. She absently fingers the curved contour of the toque.

Over the span of fifty years, Lynn and Dorothy have brought in about six hundred thousand bushels of soybeans between them while Flora scribbled across as many pages and plowed through a swamp's worth of El Dorado rum. "If that girl had been a Holstein," Father had said, "we'd have sent her out for veal."

"Don't go fiddling with the toque, Lynn. Her blood'll make a mess of your hands."

Lynn looks to her now-moist fingertips and is unsettled to discover that she has halfway removed the toque from Flora's head.

"Leave it be," Dorothy says. "Wore the thing for most of her goddamn life. Guess we should bury her in it."

Lynn brings her face close to the ground, inhales deeply of the damp wool, and thinks of Mother. She remembers Mother's calloused fingers and how they had coaxed loop upon rosy loop over cackling needle tips while she knitted the toques. When her work was through, Mother had run those same fingers through the nest of Flora's matted hair, and had sat for an hour trying to untangle her before placing the toque on her head. She had never had to do that for Lynn, though. Lynn knows how to use a goddamn brush, doesn't she?

Lynn reaches deep into her mind and pulls out a memory of her childhood self. In it, she is wearing her own pink toque and calling for little Flora to come outside. Now the two of them are shrieking with a joy that is jarring to recall, and their heads are winding like whorls of cotton candy as they roll down the snow-packed slope of the drive. The memory is surreal, and it blinds Lynn like sudden sunlight. She considers the woman she is now, the girl she was then, and the fifty years of driving parallel lines across a bean field that she has put between them.

"Do you think she's with her, Dorothy?"

"What?"

"Flora. With Mother."

"Hell, Lynn," Dorothy says as she takes a step backward. "Don't spin loose on us now."

Dorothy gives Flora's arm another nudge with her boot heel, and this time it meets with sufficient resistance. Dorothy fishes her cellphone out of her jeans and starts to walk away.

"Gonna go out to the east field. Better reception."

Lynn feels something inside her start to unravel, and she brings her lips in close to Flora's ear. She pets the moist tendrils of Flora's hair and whispers, "What do you see out there, Florrie? Eh? Eh?"

Lynn lifts her eyes to search for Dorothy's receding figure, but Dorothy has become lost in the sea of shorn beanstalks in the east field. The pinkish wisps of the coming day dance across the sky as a distant siren drifts in from the west. Lynn's hands skate across the slick crimson surface of the once-pink toque. Two cents a yard. No sense griping about the colour. Lynn pries the toque from Flora's bloody scalp and slides it snug over her own. It fits just fine.

The siren bleats louder as Lynn lays herself beside Flora and stares upward. She watches the storm gather above them, and it is barely a moment before Lynn feels the first snowflakes begin to dissolve on her cheeks. Lynn runs her tongue over her lips, and there, hidden within the dry crevices of her salty skin, is the subtle taste of sugar. Laughter bubbles from Lynn's throat as she stretches her arms out straight as arrows and starts to roll down the slope.

Swirls of pink on grey churn around her as she turns, and although she doesn't yet see it, Lynn can tell there is a lion prowling above her, just waiting for the candied clouds to coalesce and reveal its majestic form.

When she reaches the bottom of the drive, the sun crests the tree line and fires its rays straight through Lynn's pupils. She closes her eyes tight and brings her hands forward to touch the fire that has started to burn just below her breastbone.

Beneath Lynn's closed lids, the sunlight remains.

Lynn feels Mother's rough fingers as they begin to criss-cross the even rows of her fuchsia toque.

The incoming siren's sound is swallowed into the maelstrom of the sudden snowsquall, and everything goes quiet. Lynn leans her head back into Mother's hands, and a new sound falls upon her cooling ears. From across the bean stocks, out past the horizon, and somewhere deep in the north woods, Lynn hears Flora calling for her.

"Come outside," Flora whispers. "Sister, come outside."

Norma's Fire

Shirley drives Norma bonkers, but that's what happens after fifty years, three car accidents, and a lifetime of watching *The Price Is Right*.

There are things she loves about Shirley, like how the old doll can play thirty-six speed bingo cards at once when Norma can only do sixteen. That's something.

Then there's the way Shirley's got a comeback for everything. When the dip from the cosmetics counter tries to sell her a twelve-dollar lipstick, Shirley looks right up into her thick-mascaraed eyes and says, "Honey, makeup don't fix stupidity."

You can't teach that kind of sass. You've gotta be born with it.

Nothing's ever perfect though, and the thing that crawls right under Norma's skin is Shirley's fussing. Shirley doesn't gripe about the big stuff; she can't even tell you the name of the Prime Minister. It's the little things that set her off.

One time, they're out on the back porch, ready to enjoy a gin, smoke, and their daily fix of television's most exciting hour of fantastic prizes, when Shirley starts going off about the gas fireplace.

"Didya turn off the flame, Norma? Didya? Didya?"

Norma's tempted to tell Shirley to get off her own goddamn arse and check, but she doesn't, on account of Shirley's bad knee and the simple fact that'd be no way to speak to your wife.

Another time they're getting ready to dig into a fresh bowl of summer cherries and Shirley says, "Didya remember to wash these, Norma? Didya? Didya?"

Norma steams up and says, "Course I did, Shirl, waddaya take me for?"

"One L short of normal is what."

Norma kicks herself because she should've seen that one coming.

She knows Shirley isn't gonna leave it, so she runs every one of those red devils under the faucet again just to button her up.

Shirley likes to go on about how Norma is losing her marbles, but Norma knows the problem isn't her. The problem is Shirley and her sizzling nerves.

Norma tries to stay patient, tries to focus on the good points of Shirley, but today might just be the day it all breaks down.

They're halfway to bingo when Shirley starts up about the stove.

"Didya remember to turn it off, Norma? Didya? Didya?"

Ten minutes late for Lucky Tuesday and the old bird wants to turn the car around.

Norma feels the flames lick the insides of her nostrils and takes the left turn a little fast. The car starts to drift, and Shirley grips the door handle tight.

Hasn't got a comeback now, has she? Has she?

Then Norma looks at Shirley's terrified eyes and tells herself she's taking things too far. Shirley might be a harpy, but she's all Norma's got.

Norma rights the car and says, "Chrissakes, Shirley. I checked the son of a bitch 'fore we left, it weren't on."

But she hadn't.

And it was.

Plastered

Trouble follows Lyla.

"Like the tail follows the ass," says Arlon. He stands in the yard grinning, three teeth gone, the black hollow of this throat peeking through the gaps.

"Time to go," says the big-mouthed cop who is there to escort Arlon off the property. Arlon is not in favour of the divorce, and he's stopped by to demonstrate the depth of his displeasure.

All the cops in Victoria County won't be able to keep Arlon away for long, and the three of them know it. As soon as Lyla fixes the goddamn wall, she'll have to put on her boots and start walking.

Lyla locks eyes with the cop for about half a second, but it's enough time to realize he couldn't care less about any of it. Just doing his job.

"Later, darlin'," says Arlon as he tips the brim of his ball cap and fixes Lyla with a smile so sweet it is sinister.

Lyla passes the hallway mirror on the way back inside and stares past the shiner under her eye. It's time to forget about that now. Instead, she searches her reflection for some sign of the strong-headed woman she used to be, back in the good years, back before she moved to Grand Forks and trouble found her. The lines around Lyla's mouth look as if they were drawn there by a burrowing wood-worm and her hair hangs limp around the sag of her chin.

"Too damn old to be starting from zip," she mutters to her reflection. But Lyla knows, come tomorrow, that's just what she will have to do.

The hole in the wall is about two feet across. When Lyla had shown the house, she'd shoved the dresser in front of it and nobody had been the wiser – but tomorrow is closing day. She can't risk a wrinkle, not with Arlon circling the nest. She needs every penny. Her half of this house and the shitty Camry in the yard are all she will get out of the divorce. They're all that stands between her and some dipshit cousin's couch.

Lyla cracks open a king can of Bud, leans against the dresser, and runs her fingers across the uneven edges of the hole. It's an old house, double brick construction, thick walls. "Good bones" is what her real estate agent had written in the listing.

Arlon, who had grown up surrounded by hot tempers and dry-wall, had been unpleasantly surprised the first time he slammed his fist against the wall and came up against two inches of solid plaster.

Three smashed hand bones, but the ass wouldn't stand down. Arlon had grabbed a hammer and come straight back up to smash the mother through. That's how things always went with Arlon. Didn't like anything that stood up to him.

Lyla opens her banged-up laptop, logs on to YouTube, and searches for a tutorial on repairing plaster. She scrolls down through a few screens of middle-aged cowboys in tool belts until she finds a link for Dykes with Drills®. Lyla is not lesbian, but she is tired of men telling her what to do.

She clicks the link and listens to a woman named Patty tell her how a hole is always bigger than you think, and you've got to keep digging till you find the solid edges. "It can seem intimidating at first," Patty says as the video ticks forward on the screen, "but it's better to know what you're dealing with so there are no surprises."

Lyla examines the side of her beer can and considers the possible downsides of using power tools while she is this drunk. She's been trying to cut down and had a pretty good dry spell going before this last blowout. The older Lyla gets, the less she can handle her drinking. It's true what Arlon says: trouble always follows her. She takes a swig of the Bud.

"Let's fire this up," says Patty through the glowing screen.

Lyla hesitates but tells herself she is not exactly wading through a puddle of other options. So, she'll have at the wall. It feels good to make a simple decision. It is a feeling she had almost forgotten after twenty years of living under Arlon's thumb.

A call comes through on her cellphone, so Lyla puts Patty, and the moment of truth, on pause. The call is from Minerva, the last in the long line of Lyla's friends she figured had given up on her. It's been ages since they last spoke, and Lyla wonders what, here in the eleventh hour, the old bitch could want? She decides not to answer.

Lyla remembers what it felt like to talk to someone she wasn't wholly afraid of. She thinks of how she would sit out under the crabapple tree, surrounded by the smell of booze and overripe fruit, and listen to Minerva rip apart everyone in town. One night, when they were especially gone, Minerva had pointed her beer can over the top of the house, turned to Lyla, and said, "You ever get the feeling that someone is just watching over us, just laughing their damn asses off at the mess we've made of ourselves?" Lyla hadn't known how to answer, so she'd just cracked the next king can and waited for the moment to pass. But it had felt good to be understood by someone, even someone like Minerva.

Lyla runs her palm across the edge of her forearm. She notes how her bone has healed completely now. She remembers the price she paid at Arlon's hand for that last evening of unsatisfying buzzing with Minerva, remembers sitting on the stretcher with some cooked-up story about how she'd fallen out of the tree. Doc Preston had known Lyla long enough to know she was lying, but he hadn't cared much. He just did his job and quietly reset her bone. "Trouble is your twin sister, Lyla" was all he'd said.

But still, she liked the way he had assembled her cast, wound the plaster slowly like he was wrapping something precious, then smoothed it flush against her skin like a summer sheet on a mattress.

After the phone stops ringing, Lyla downs the last of her beer and presses the small triangle covering Patty's eager face. Lyla gathers her bottom lip beneath her two front teeth and holds the hammer high.

"Don't be afraid to get a little aggressive," says Patty. "No matter what's under there, just dig it out, and I'll show you how to fix it in episode three." Lyla considers the deformed wall and takes a quick look back to Patty, who is standing in someone's living room, crowbar in hand: the handywoman hero of Red Deer.

"Do what you need to do," Patty says.

"Ya better not be shittin' me, Pat," Lyla says to the screen as she holds her hammer frozen in position. She waits for Patty to answer but then remembers she is only a recording.

"Gotten nuttier than butter, woman," Lyla tells herself and drives her hammer into the wall.

She smashes hard against the edges of the hole, and it caves in like a rotten squash. When the initial thrill of her action has subsided, Lyla starts to lose heart. She considers the damage. Her breath comes in short bursts from the exertion, and she stops hammering. Patty's voice thunders through the dust cloud. "Make sure you get right in there, friend. There are no mistakes that can't be fixed."

Lyla likes how Patty calls her "friend." It's been a while since Lyla has considered herself anything other than someone's "problem of a wife." Lyla also likes how it feels when she breaks apart the wall, the sensation of something yielding beneath her.

The laths peek out from behind the plaster, all equally spaced like the bars of a wooden cage. Unsure of what comes next, Lyla turns back to the computer.

"Once you're sure you've got everything, it's time to move on to episode two: mixing plaster," says Patty.

But Lyla isn't ready for episode two. Something is wrong. She slides her dusty finger across the keyboard and pauses the video. A heaviness circles Lyla and all the air seems to disappear from the room. The plaster particles pause, suspended in mid-flight, and hang before her, still as dense fog. Then, from somewhere deep inside the house, Lyla hears a distant moan. The sky outside shifts and sunbeams beat in from the west-facing window. Then the wind starts. Luminous white lines of swirling matter churn around Lyla's body – a tornado of plaster dust that has chosen her as its centre.

A chill creeps across Lyla's arms and she draws them closer to her chest. Then, as quickly as it started, the churning ceases.

Lyla takes a tentative step toward the hole. It is now four feet across. The disturbance threatens again, and Lyla realizes the wind is coming from inside the wall.

Lyla lays a hand flat against wall struts and presses the place where one of them has broken. The strut gives way and permits Lyla's hand to pass through into the space beyond. She feels air flutter through her fingers and pulls her hand back inside the bedroom.

Lyla closes her eyes and forces her head forward into the darkness. Her upper body enters the space beyond the broken wall while her feet remain planted in the bedroom floor. She opens her eyes and finds herself staring into nothing. A calm overtakes her as she inhales deeply of the stale black air. Her eyes adjust, and Lyla sees the space is more extensive than she'd expected. The floorboards continue inward – past the struts – until they stop at the edge of another plaster wall, three feet deeper than the one where she's standing. *It's strange*, thinks Lyla. *Like a room behind a room.*

Lyla sees something lying on the enclosed floor and squints to bring the thing into focus. Her eyes trace the chalky edges of a femur, the spread fan of a ribcage, and above it, a skull.

"Human, for sure," Lyla whispers to the space. She feels only numbness in response to this gruesome find. *The life I've lived*, she thinks. *I guess I can take my horrors in stride.*

Lyla extends her neck and lowers her face closer to the skeleton.

"What's the story here, bones?" she asks.

Her eyes fall to the skeleton's hand, its bones carelessly splayed behind the skull of this newfound trouble. There, skewered through its centre by a slender fingerbone, lies a ring.

Lyla runs her fingertips across the dry surface of the bones and then closes them around the perimeter of the ring. She wiggles the ring loose, careful not to disturb the delicate structures that it surrounds.

Lyla retreats from the hole and inspects the ring in the light of the bedroom. There is an inscription on its inner surface, and she can just make out the words: *Edward 1939*. The ring is small, and Lyla slips it onto her fourth finger. Perfect fit. She thinks of this man named Edward and wonders what kind of woman he might have married.

"I'll bet it was him who put ya here, eh, friend?" she says.

"It's a bottom fact," says a voice from inside the wall. "Now be a peach and give me back my ring."

The voice has a canned quality to it, like an actress from one of the old radio shows Lyla's grandma used to listen to back home.

The gust from the hidden room grows stronger, and Lyla sits back onto the floor. She removes the ring from her finger and tries to focus. Fighting her way through a haze of drink, Lyla tells herself that the voice is simply a product of her pickled mind. There've been a few things happening lately that she's been unsure of, and Lord knows her liver has been getting worse. "Sorry," Lyla says, just in case.

"Never mind," says the voice. Drunk or not, there's no denying it this time. "I'll come out there and get it myself."

The sun from the west-facing window flickers, and a shadow passes across Patty's face, frozen on the computer screen. When the voice speaks again, it does so from inside the bedroom.

"Actually, you can keep it. You've still got all your skin on, haven't you? It's probably more use to you than me. No sense wasting good gold. Won't be worth anything where I'm going, and you can take *it* to the bank and cash it in."

Lyla turns to the place beside the window where the voice seems to have drifted.

"Where ya going to?" asks Lyla, feeling more peaceful than she knows she ought to.

"To the angels, I imagine," says the voice. "That's where all the sweethearts like us go. Lord, what I wouldn't give for a shot of whatever you're drinking before I go."

Lyla is pleased that the voice seems ready to include her. She's tired of always being on the outside of things.

"Have ya been in here the whole time?" asks Lyla.

"In the walls, you mean? Why, yes. I was just waiting there for *ages* for you to spring me."

"Why didn't ya come out before? Can't see that plaster having kept ya back. Must've had a curse on ya or something. Maybe cuz of what he did to ya. Ya think?"

"How should I know?" says the voice. "I don't make the rules. I'm only obliged to follow them. What I do know is it's an absolute *smash* to be out here in the open. And by the way, what have you done to my bedroom?"

"Don't have much money," Lyla says.

"Don't need both my eyes to see that," says the voice.

The voice seems to be coming closer.

"Willikers, honey, what happened to your face?" says the voice.

Lyla touches the swelling below her right eye, and her spirits sink. She's been enjoying talking to this new friend, whoever she is, and is afraid to bring trouble back into the room.

"Oh, peas and carrots," the voice continues. "I don't know why I'm even asking. Course, it was *him* who did it. I guess we both know a few shakes about picking a bad man, now don't we?"

Lyla hears the sound of her own laughter rise from her throat, and it's a queer sound, at once forgotten and familiar.

"Right on there, Mrs. Edward," Lyla says.

"Oh, nonsense, call me Agnes," says the voice. "Spent my whole grown life attached to that devil. I'll be damned if I spend my after-years dragging him around by my ankle."

"But ya seem so cheerful," says Lyla. "For someone who got done in by their man."

"Well, you know as well as I do how a thing like that can consume you, but it's amazing the holes you can think yourself out of with eighty years and nothing else to occupy your mind," says Agnes.

"Some things ya just can't get past," says Lyla.

"It's true, and it isn't," says Agnes. "There's no denying the horror of it, Lyla, the damage it does. But I guess I decided not to let it consume me, see?"

"But how could ya help it?"

"There's little sprouts inside you that can take root when they've got the right soil to stretch out in," says Agnes.

Lyla feels pleasure building as Agnes speaks. *Agnes,* Lyla thinks. *Now there's a pretty sort of name for a friend.*

"Why, thank you, Lyla," says Agnes. "It was my mother's name too."

But the warm feeling is short-lived. It isn't long before the implications of Agnes's existence shower Lyla like a sudden hailstorm.

Human bones, however old, are sure to throw a wrench in the closing. Lyla's heard somewhere that a murder-house can expect a twenty to thirty percent drop in resale value, to say nothing of the damage or lost time that'll come from any investigation.

Lyla wipes her cheeks with the back of her hand as the plaster dust mixes with her budding tears.

"I see where your thoughts are pointed, Lyla," Agnes says as her voice crosses back toward the dresser. "But it couldn't be simpler, see?"

"What the hell is simple about me finding yer old bones in my house walls on the day before I was planning to skip town?" Lyla mumbles.

"Oh, don't be glum," Agnes says, her voice moving back and forth across the room as if she is pacing. "I can't *stand* you when you're moody. Just be happy you found me once I was all dried up. Imagine the sight eighty years ago? Now *that* might've been enough to shake up even the likes of you. Besides, I went easy on you, didn't I? Didn't even *try* to scare you. I don't mind saying I have some sympathy for you because of that Arlon fella you've had to bear. Part of me wishes it had been *him* that busted me out fifteen years back. He almost did, too. Remember? Well, I'll tell you one thing, that meeting, had it happened, might not have been quite so congenial."

"Whadaya mean?" Lyla asks.

"I probably don't look much to you now …. " Agnes's voice is still for a moment. "Say, Lyla, can you see me at all?"

"Nope. Only hear yer voice," Lyla says.

"What a shame. The dress I'm wearing is to die for. Ha! You get it? Anyway, it's a mint green number with a Chantilly trim. Lotta blood on it, to be sure, but still, it's an absolute dream."

"But what were ya saying before? About scaring off my Arlon?" Lyla says.

"I knew that would pique your interest, Miss L. Not nearly as dead inside as you act now, are you?"

"Go ahead. What would ya have done?"

Agnes's voice returns the window as she says, "Oh, sweetheart! You would have loved it. I'd have set him on fire before a shriek had even left his mouth. I've been itching to get out here for years so that I could fix that Jekyll right up for you. Never could figure why you didn't stand up to him."

"Ya ever stand up to Mr. Edward, Agnes?" Lyla asks.

"Guess I did, honey, and look where that got me. So maybe you had the right idea after all. Waited till he did enough to get the police involved, didn't you? Smart. Thing is, Lyla, in my day, the police wouldn't help a woman like they do today."

"Haven't found them to be too helpful," Lyla says.

Thinking of the police, Lyla remembers how she has work to do and she had better get to it. Lyla looks upward to the computer screen, to Patty's patient face, and to the promise of mixed plaster.

"Listen, Agnes," Lyla says, "would ya mind if I just left ya in there? Like covered over the wall, and Bob's yer uncle? It'd sure help me with the closing."

The wind picks up again, and Lyla hears Agnes's voice right beside her cheek.

"I won't hear of it, Lyla. No, ma'am. I'm attached to those bones until someone puts them underground, and that someone, Lyla, is gonna be you."

Lyla sees her neat solution dissolve in front of her, thinks of a parade of ratty couches stretching out into infinity, and starts to panic.

"What if I do cover it over, Agnes? You'll have to go back, won't ya? I mean, something made ya stay in there in the first place."

"You can try," Agnes says with a new edge to her voice that Lyla doesn't like, "but I'll tell you, honey, it won't be pretty."

Lyla lowers her head to her knees and exhales. *The trouble with me*, Lyla thinks, *is that I can't say no to anyone.*

"Now that's a lie if I ever head one," says Agnes. "Arlon didn't want the divorce, now did he?"

"Didn't think I would go through with it. Wasn't sure myself until I signed the papers."

"And that's what got him riled up, isn't it?" Agnes says.

"He don't like to be wrong."

"Didn't feel like sleeping in jail tonight either, I'll bet. You surprised the hell out of both of us when you called the police."

"I guess."

"Well, those are some pretty significant noes in my book," Agnes says. "You've got to give yourself more credit. Focus on your strong points."

Lyla sits forward, rests her elbows on the floor, and holds her face in her hands. "Could ya really have burned him up, Agnes?" Lyla asks.

"Sure as I'm standing here," says Agnes. "Look out the window there and I'll show you. You see that dead old crabapple in the yard – planted it myself, did you know that?"

"Can't say I did," Lyla says.

"Damn straight," says Agnes. "Now get an eyeful of this."

There is a flash of light outside the window, followed by the smell of burning wood. Lyla stands, shuffles to the window, and watches as the crabapple tree crumbles into flames.

"Wow, Agnes," says Lyla. "I would die to be able to do something like that."

"Careful what you wish for, honey," says Agnes. "You can do more than you know. You only need to learn how to steer your own horse."

"Me and my friend Minerva used to sit under that tree and drink," says Lyla.

"I'll tell you one thing about that Minerva," says Agnes. "She's not your friend."

"Ya know something I don't, Agnes?" Lyla asks, but in her heart, she already knows what Agnes will say.

"She was just trying to pull you backward into her rum pond so she'd have someone to swim with, and you goddamn know it," Agnes says. "Your friend Patty on the screen there, now she's the real deal. A true friend helps you to help yourself, is what I always say."

Lyla looks to the computer screen as Patty's face dissolves into a screensaver.

"Patty is something else, right?" says Lyla as she crosses to the computer and jiggles the touchpad.

"Imagine having yer shit together like that?" Lyla says as Patty's face reappears. "Yer own YouTube channel? Fix anything ya want to? It'd be friggin' paradise."

Lyla looks to the wall and examines it with despair.

"Look at that, Agnes," she says. "How the hell am I ever gonna fix that?"

Lyla feels a coolness creep across her left shoulder, and Agnes's voice speaks directly into her right ear. "It'll get worse before it gets better, Lyla. But you heard what our Patty told you: you don't need to be afraid."

Lyla puts the Camry in drive and coasts down the driveway. Who would have thought it could be so easy? Yesterday she was alone, intoxicated, and covered in plaster. Today she's sober, eighty grand richer, with a full tank of gas to boot. The only thing left for her to do is get out of Victoria County.

As she cruises down the side road, Lyla thinks of the covered hole in a wall she no longer owns, filled in by her own hands after six episodes of Dykes with Drills®, four private messages, and two phone calls to her new friend Patty in Red Deer.

As Lyla glides to a rolling stop at the edge of town, she remembers how delicate the plaster had felt under her palms as she smoothed it over a final time, just before she painted over the wall.

"Shoulda been a doctor, I guess," she says to the interior of the car.

Lyla thinks of the kilometres between here and Red Deer, all five thousand of them. She is unsure if it will be enough distance to put between her and Arlon, but she'll give it a shot. As she coasts through the next intersection, her cellphone rings, and, on a whim, Lyla puts it on speaker. Minerva's voice fills the car.

"Been trying to call you for months, you old cow," says Minerva. "Come on over and have a few with me, won't you?"

"Don't think I will, Min," Lyla says, and she looks to the passenger seat beside her. There sits her shiny new suitcase, packed up so tight the latches wouldn't even close. "I'm tryin' to cut down," she says into the air.

"That's a laugh," says Minerva. "You're in deeper than I am, and that's something. You try to go off it, you'll be scrambled eggs with a side of hash."

"Gotta go now, Minnie."

The line goes silent, and Lyla wonders if Minerva has gone. Suddenly, a new voice fills the interior of the car. "You jest remember, Lyla," says Arlon, "that trouble follows ye."

The line goes dead.

Right on cue come the flashing lights in Lyla's rear-view mirror. Lyla thinks about gunning it, just trying to take a runner on the whole situation, but the more she considers it, the more she realizes she has to face things as they are.

Just her luck, when the cop approaches the window, it's old Big Tooth from yesterday, and Lyla can tell by the way he's looking past her that she will get just as much sympathy from him as Arlon had.

"Got you rolling through the stop sign back there, ma'am," says Toothy as he peers into the car.

"I'll take the ticket gladly," Lyla says, but then realizes she sounds too eager. Toothy turns his face sideways like he's just caught the scent of something, and his eyes fall on the suitcase where it gleams on the passenger seat.

"What's in the case, lady?" asks Toothy, "You goin' on a trip somewhere?"

The temperature rockets up several degrees inside the Camry, and Lyla feels like she might choke. She opens her mouth but cannot think of anything to say. She can already see the film reel of what happens next rolling out down the road in front of her.

Something explodes behind Toothy, and the awful sound is followed by a whoosh that sucks all the air out of the Camry.

"Holy shit, officer," Lyla says, looking in her side mirror. "What the hell just happened to yer cruiser?"

"Jesus H. Christ," Toothy says as he unclips his walkie-talkie from his vest and breaks into a run. Toothy has almost reached the cruiser by the time the dime drops in Lyla's mind, and she begins to cackle.

"Would you, for the love of liberty, get this car on the road before he thinks to ask any more questions?' says Agnes. "It's fifty hours I'm obliged to ride with this goddamn suitcase, and I'm not inclined to make it more."

"Like I told ya, Agnes," says Lyla. "I'll take ya to the back-woods out past the falls if ya want me to."

"No dice, darling. I'm along for the ride wherever you're going. Spent my whole damn life in Victoria County, gonna get out a little and see the world."

Lyla puts the car in gear and slides it back onto the road.

"And you've got to be snappier with your comebacks," continues Agnes, "if you want to get us all the way to Alberta without anyone poking around this bag and landing the both of us behind bars."

Lyla's confidence tries to waver, but she fights it back. "I hope we make it, Agnes," Lyla says. "Patty says Red Deer is a beaut of a city. What I'm afraid of, though, is – "

"Oh, *he* won't find us, honey. Don't get your knickers in a knot," says Agnes. "And if he does, you *know* it'll be a hot day for him in hell."

Lyla looks in the rear-view mirror at the distant glow on the receding roadside.

"Uh-huh," says Agnes. "You got my number, Lyla."

Lyla smiles, reaches past the gearshift, and slides her hand across to the slippery surface of the suitcase.

Madame and Yves

Pomorski and his insidious papers present an unforeseen obstacle to The Roach's mission.

"Okey-doke, Yves. All set up for booth M18. Just sign here, please and thank you, and welcome to Sprouts of Spring Craft Show."

The Roach looks uneasily at the entrance of the warehouse.

"Have you assigned a place to Madame Mantis?"

"Mandy Hagopian? She's not here yet."

The Roach's relief is palpable.

"You will assign her to the booth across from mine, like last year."

The Roach slides a red fifty across the registration desk, and a sinister smile crosses Pomorski's face.

"Yves, you old dog."

The Roach's eyes are sharp behind thick-lensed glasses. He is alert for the appearance of Madame Mantis. He runs his hands over the smooth surface of his wares; upcycled leather bags with seat belt clips. Each bag is hand-inked and bears the image of a superhero of The Roach's creation.

The Roach's hand comes to rest on the largest and most intricate of the bags. The muscled green thighs of Madame Mantis leap from the leather, as if she might break free from her inky prison and surround him with her powerful limbs. The product of a mating between a plant-man and a mantis, she is mistress of the garden and the woman of The Roach's dreams.

Madame Mantis, wrapped majestically in a size twenty-four emerald peacoat, approaches the registration table and prepares to do battle.

"Name?"

"You know who I am."

Pomorski petulantly checks his list and circles a name with his cheap red pen.

"Huh. Mandy Hagopain. M25, right across from Yves again. People may talk."

Pomorski's gaze roves over Madame Mantis's impressive form.

"But maybe you are no longer capable of human love."

Madame Mantis slams her fist on the table and shakes it to its plywood core.

Pomorski's eyes dart from the meatiness of her clenched fingers to the line of artisans forming behind her. His voice carries through the warehouse like a shrill bird's.

"Next in line!"

Madame Mantis bounds down aisle M in a rage. Her bulging arms expand by the second and strain the sleeves of her peacoat to the point of bursting. Several artisans stare openly as she passes, intrigued by her transformation. Madame Mantis tells herself to ignore them. They are jealous of her new form. With great power comes immense loneliness, but Madame Mantis has her plan. She can have it all.

She gathers her enormous coat around her so her meta-morphosis will be less apparent. The problem with the change is the anger that comes with it. Her darker nature, always difficult to harness, has come closer to the surface. Madame Mantis can no longer predict when she will turn.

"Staring problems, people?" Madame Mantis sweeps forward to face her accusers and the hem of her emerald coat flares.

"Uh ... no, Mandy. Sorry."

The artisans scatter and return to the shadows of their booths.

Madame Mantis tosses her head like a jungle cat, and her eyes meet those of the last man standing in her wake. Suddenly, The Roach and Madame Mantis are transported back to this time and place one year ago, and the memory of their first and last conversation.

Madame Mantis had approached the table and perused The Roach's offerings with the cool disdain of a grade school principal.

"Are these real leather?"

The Roach's silence had been his answer.

"There is only one woman at your table."

The Roach, puzzled, had turned his eyes downward to where Madame Mantis's finger had rested on a small sketch of a green insect lady, lost in a sea of muscled men.

"Sexist much, Mr. Roche?"

The Roach shakes his head to free himself from the physical pain of the memory. His power diminished, he takes shelter behind his painted sign.

'R. Yves Roche – Upcycled Leather Satchels.'

Madame Mantis assembles her booth and The Roach observes her from behind the pages of his comic book.

Madame Mantis's hair is luminous and falls in thick black curls that reach halfway down the back of her emerald coat. The Roach dabs the corner of his mouth with a napkin and waits for her to turn around. He brings his fingers to his lips and counts all the things he knows about Madame Mantis.

His hearing is keen and The Roach has learned much from his four years of eavesdropping across aisle M. Madame Mantis lives in a basement apartment in Cabbagetown. She likes plants better than people. Her ex-boyfriend is a weakling who hung her out to dry because he couldn't stand up to her strong personality.

Madame Mantis lays eight long trays across her table and coats them with a thin layer of iridescent sand. Atop the sand she arranges clay pots shaped like hands with palms up and fingers slightly splayed. Each pot holds a single bonsai tree, pruned to perfection.

The Roach's comic book slips closer to his table as he considers Madame Mantis's fluid movements and the way her cat-eye glasses frame her solid, Armenian nose.

Miniature ultraviolet lights appear on her table. All are uniquely crafted in a retro-atomic style to resemble an iconic preying insect. The elegant mantises illuminate each bonsai like a spotlight. The effect takes The Roach's breath away.

The Roach's comic book falls from his hand and clatters to the floor. Madame Mantis turns her head, and he drinks in a moment of her angry stare.

She clips a sign to the front of her table and steps back to assess her efforts.

The Roach can recite the words of her sign from memory. He often whispers them to the dark walls of his solitary apartment.

"Madame Mantis, Gardens for Darkness."

The Roach says the words to himself, under his breath like an incantation.

Madame Mantis walks to her booth, sits heavily, and shrugs her emerald coat onto her chair.

A bearish woman approaches The Roach's table.

"Do you have Superman? My grandson likes Superman."

The Roach is taken aback by the strength of the woman's perfume and the chartreuse slather of her eyeshadow.

"No. He's the least compelling superhero, in my opinion. Have you considered Razorhyde? Here he is. You see, ma'am? He has the head of a swine."

Madame Mantis's voice drifts across the aisle as she addresses her own customer. The Roach drinks in her melody.

"That's it, ma'am, botany and energy fused," she says. "Light as beauty and life where there should be none. Perfect for the underground dweller."

The Roach leans his face on his moist palm and pretends Madame Mantis is speaking directly to him.

"Oh my! I'm afraid it's all too space age for me!"

Madame Mantis presents her middle finger to the customer's disappearing form.

The Roach feasts on her fierceness and she senses his attention. Without adjusting the position of her fingers, she rotates her hand to face him.

Under the heat of her gaze, the Roach recalls his mission. He grabs the largest bag from his table and stands. Madame Mantis rises in unison, perceiving his action as retaliatory to her rude gesture.

A new reality dawns as Madame Mantis's stomach comes into view. Without the veil of her emerald coat, it protrudes in front of her, and points menacingly across aisle M. The crumbling wall of The Roach's expectation falls heavily on his soul.

The Roach looks despondently at Madame Mantis's gravid state and realizes who he really is. He is no superhero in waiting. He is a yesterday's man selling bags made of trash.

Like a sucker punch perfectly executed, Pomorski ambles up to The Roach's table and leans in like they're closing a deal.

"Hey, Yves. Give you some advice about old Mandy. She's a go-er but, dude, that temper is something else. When that bomb goes off you don't want to be anywhere near the place."

Both men fail to notice Madame Mantis's approach. She kicks the base of The Roach's table with her powerful leg and the seat belt clasps rattle.

"Do you have something to say to me, numbnuts?"

"Uh ... no?"

The Roach realizes too late that Madame Mantis is addressing Pomorski.

Pomorski snorts and says haughtily, "Just looking out for the safety of my exhibitors."

Madame Mantis's face reddens with rage.

"Don't test me, Jim, I swear to god ... "

"Screw you, Mandy."

Pomorski turns and bolts like a fawn, knocking Madame Mantis off balance.

The Roach reaches out to steady her and she shoves him away with great force.

"You think you're just the cat's ass, don't you? Sitting over there with your spiky hair and your edgy bags? Charming all those vapid hags and drinking up their money?"

Madame Mantis raises her hands in front of her and speaks with a terrible French accent.

"Bonjour! I'm Yves, I'm from Quebec, and I'm just so goddamn impressive to everyone!"

"But I'm not ... "

"Talking shit about me with Pomorski and snickering like a grade school thug? It's no wonder a woman can't find a proper mate in this den of bloody misogyny."

The Roach steels a glance at Madame Mantis's belly.

"You know how old I am, Yves? Thirty-eight. Thirty-eight and never had a partner who lasted more than three months. Every night I go home to my basement apartment and my goddamn garden of darkness, and I think, Mandy, there's gotta be more than this!"

"What about your husband?"

"What is this, 1953? Jesus. I went and spent twelve thousand bucks I didn't have on in vitro because guess what, Yves? Nobody is interested in mating with a tough-ass Armenian girl with a bad temper!"

"So your child is fatherless?"

"Is that all you heard out of everything I just said?"

Madame Mantis's eyes mist over and The Roach hovers a hand over her shoulder. He is somewhere between vomiting and a heart attack. Madame Mantis gives his hand a slap and snickers.

"Hands off, Roche. It's not time for a hero show just because a girl has a moment. Go back to your table, Superman, and leave the rest of us mortals alone."

The Roach reddens and retreats to his table. He grips the large bag in both of his trembling hands and breathes hard. A button in the middle of his shirt pops free from the abrupt expansion of his chest. His brain screams and starts to pound against his skull. The Roach knows this will end badly, but he is powerless against his dark rage. He bounds back to Madame Mantis with the ferocity of a recently freed gorilla. He bangs the bag down on the table and the miniature insect lights flicker.

"See that? I made it for you. See her? That's Madame Mantis. The only girl at my goddamn table. She's one of the most powerful and, screw it, I'm just gonna say it, *sexy* heroines in fair trade, non-toxic ink!"

The Roach's eyes catch fire and the inside of his skin turns green.

Madame Mantis takes a step backward and draws a sharp breath as the Roach's rage crests.

"Maybe if you'd been willing to have this conversation a year ago you wouldn't have had to waste all your money on IVF!"

The weight of the Roach's statement pauses the world long enough for the surroundings to come back in to focus.

The Roach feels the first tendrils of retreat pulling at his heels.

The two heroes stand alone in aisle M with only the sound of their ragged breath between them.

Madame Mantis's eyes dance hungrily over The Roach as if she might consume him.

The Roach jerks his foot forward and shakes something loose.

He floods his lungs with the hot air between them and says, "Maybe when you're done giving birth, we can go for coffee."

"I'm not due till the seventeenth."

"Oh."

"What are you doing tomorrow?"

Sheila's Mine

Sam runs her tongue across the uneven suture line that holds together her bottom lip. She licks the ferrous edges and thinks about the sound her mandible made when it cracked against Havier's errant shovel. She remembers the snap, sudden looseness of her mouth, and the puddle of salt and iron that oozed forth to fill the space. She considers the speed with which things can be broken and fixed. She'd started her shift at the Tullared Mine with an intact jaw, and in the span of a few hours it has been both dislocated and forced back into its socket.

Against everyone's advice, Sam had driven herself to the emergency room. She acted fast and left her colleagues no choice. In times of vulnerability, Sam likes to take things immediately into her own hands. She is easily overwhelmed by the well-meaning input of others.

Sam checks the clock on the dashboard as she slides herself behind the wheel of her truck. It is only four fifteen. She exhales. She will easily make it home in time and her sister, Sheila will remain unaffected by this strange perturbation in their daily routine. Since their mother died, Sam has never been late for Sheila. She isn't sure what would happen if she ever was, but she doesn't want to find out. Sam thinks of Sheila and wonders, like she always does, if her sister loves her. The answer has never been

90

clear. What she does know is that Sheila depends on her, and most days that is enough.

Sam starts the truck, eases out of the hospital parking lot, and fires up the radio. The announcer says ten men are trapped in the Tullared Mine. The broadcast cuts to a sound bite of Marjorie, who works in the mine's office: "I thought it was thunder," says the distant voice of the secretary, "but they weren't calling for rain, so I looked out the window. That's when I heard the siren."

Sam thinks of the six kitten statues with moving paws that sit on Marjorie's desk, how the last kitten always waves a little slower than the rest. As she thinks this thought, Sam takes her foot off the gas. The truck drifts to a gradual stop and comes to rest on a flat stretch of road before the hill.

Sam is the eleventh miner on the day shift. The shaft must have collapsed while she was at the hospital.

Eventually a car drives up behind her and lays on the horn as it swerves around her. Sam returns to earth, presses the gas, and starts to drive up the hill.

When she pulls into Tullared, she blows past the gang of reporters who have assembled at the mine's entrance and heads over to a patch of dirt out beyond the parking lot.

She is not like Sheila, but Sam sometimes does odd things when she is under stress. She kneels down beside the truck, touches her nose to the dry earth, and glides her hands over the soil. She becomes surrounded by the smell of sweat, moist rock, and dirt that she associates with being underground. The smell must be from Sam herself, but it represents all of the miners. She closes her eyes and thinks about how her team is right there underneath her. She presses her fingers one by one into the ground. Pinky is for Keith, who always brings coffee; ring is for Havier, who accidentally hit her with the shovel; middle is for Ekio, who likes to sing; index is for JoJo, who always has her back. Sam continues her count until she has named everyone who is underground, and then she starts again at the beginning.

After a while, a reporter comes over to take Sam's picture and startles Sam from her reverie. Sam looks up, sees the sun hanging low in the sky, and panics. It must be past seven. Past time for the CBC news. Past the time her big sister expects her.

Sheila. Sheila. Sheila.

Sam ignores the reporter, jumps in the truck, and by the time the loose gravel settles back onto the driveway, she is gone. She points the truck homeward, wipes back the wetness that has collected on her cheeks, and with every centimetre the sun creeps downward in her rear-view mirror, she leans harder on the gas.

The mine and everyone in it are pushed to the corners of her mind as Sam whispers Sheila's name. Her mind trembles with thoughts of her sister as Sam navigates the serpentine sideroads that lie between them. She thinks about how their evening should have gone, how it has gone each day for the past nine years, until today.

Each night, Sam returns from work at five forty-five and listens to the CBC news while Sheila arranges Mother's old spoon collection into an intricate design on the kitchen table. Sheila always finishes her work precisely at six fifteen as the anchor signs off from Edmonton. She then draws a line around the edges of the spoons with her fingertip, chuckles in her distinctive way, and rocks in time with the pendulum on their kitchen clock.

Sam remembers how she herself used to rock like Sheila, how when they were little, they pressed their shoulders together and swayed in tender waves that flowed between them. But everything had changed when the clinic had made its pronouncement: both girls affected, but Sam much less so than Sheila. After that, a gorge had opened between the sisters. Sam's had become a world of therapists, a special school, and heightened expectations, whereas Sheila had been left to hum at the table and construct her patterns. There had only been enough money for one, and the choice had been clear.

Sam knows all of Sheila's affection flows through her index finger. Before the pronouncement, back in the days before words, Sam would lie on the bed upstairs while Sheila traced the outline of Sam's small body into the sheets. Around and around Sheila would go, pressing her soft nail against the cotton fibres, rubbing them raw. Though they had never discussed it, both sisters had understood this act to be the ritual of their love.

But the more Sam had learned from the tutors, the further she had drifted from her big sister. She had started to notice how Sheila never looked at her, never stood beside her. Eventually, whenever Sam laid down on the bed, Sheila had just walked away with her hands tucked beneath her sleeves.

When Sam had learned to converse, Sheila had learned to cover her ears. When Sam had tried to touch Sheila, Sheila had started to lash out. Eventually Sam realized she had to give Sheila her space, but she continued to watch her sister from a lonely distance and hoped that one day they might float back together. Some nights, when Sheila is sleeping, Sam still lies beside her so she can feel her big sister breathe. But when morning comes, Sam always wakes up alone.

Sometimes, when her heart can stand it, Sam puts her open palm beside Sheila's spoon arrangements and hopes that Sheila will include her within the carefully traced perimeter of her love.

She never does.

Despite everything, Sam knows that if she were down in the dark rubble with all the other miners, the only thing she would be able to think about would be getting back to Sheila. Despite all that has passed between them, there is something inside Sam that pulls her back to her sister, an invisible string that refuses to break.

When Sam gets home, Sheila is not in the kitchen. The radio is tuned in to the CBC but the news is long over. The spoons are scattered like an explosion on the table and cool air spills in from the open back door. Sam calls out Sheila's name but there is no answer, only the heavy silence of an empty room.

The regular radio broadcast is interrupted to update listeners about the mine accident, but Sam does not attend to it. The methodical sound of metal striking earth beats in from the yard and is soon replaced by the racket of Sam's own shouting.

Sam races out the back door and stops short when she reaches the edge of the porch. Sheila is on the lawn, covered in mud. Surrounded by the falling night, Sheila drives her shovel into the grass with grim determination, then suddenly drops to her knees and begins to claw at the dirt.

The CBC update streams forth from inside the house. The announcer says the rescue crews have not been able to make contact with the trapped miners. Sam thinks about the spoon collection as she walks toward her sister. She imagines what the radio must have said right before the spoons had crashed onto the table's surface.

Sam squints into the dark expanse of the yard and realizes the hole Sheila is digging is already five feet deep.

Sheila raises her head like a startled rabbit and clenches her fists. Sam takes an involuntary swallow of iron-laced spit and extends an arm into the air that lies between herself and her sister. Sheila's body begins to oscillate and her breath comes in sharp bursts. Sheila looks past Sam and off toward the house as she carefully uncurls her index finger from the centre of her flexed hand.

Birds of the Falls

Mom thinks I should have made better makeup choices for our visit to Grandma's. She doesn't have to say it. I just know. She slams the car into fourth gear and darts her eyes across my face.

Normally I would call her on it, say something awful, and just let 'er rip. But despite everything, I have a slice of sympathy. It's the first anniversary of her father's death, and Mom is on her way to visit her own mother for the first time in a year. I decide to just put my feet up on the dash, roll my eyes, and let it ride.

"When are you planning to can the Bride of Frankenstein act, Chrissy?" she asks as we burn through a fresh red light. I should have known she wouldn't be able to hold it in.

"Couldn't tell you, Hillary C. Bummer about you losing the election."

My capacity for empathy is a somewhat shallow pool, but in my defense, I think it's genetic.

Mom smooths the well-sprayed edge of her hair helmet and accelerates. Her badass driving style might be the only thing she inherited from Grandpa; the rest is pure Gran. Grandpa was a working-class Romeo from Belleville, who apparently convinced my haughty grandmother to turn her back on God for the briefest of seconds, get herself knocked up, and spend the rest of her life repenting that unwise act and making those around her generally miserable.

I slap down the visor mirror, lick an errant fleck of black lipstick from my right incisor, and pull my lips back into an exaggerated snarl.

"Hey, Mom," I call across the console. "Who do I remind you of?"

Mom glances at me and says, "Your father's girlfriend?"

"Close," I say as I readjust my macabre expression in the mirror. "I'm one of Gramps's taxidermy foxes."

Mom sighs. "Try and keep a lid on it for a few hours, okay?"

I stretch my lips tighter against my teeth and emit a low growl.

"You think this is how I want to spend *my* weekend?" Mom says. "Sorting through boxes of permanently snarling beasts with my similarly humoured mother?"

"Why did he pose all of them so aggressively?" I ask. "I mean, each one of them looks ready to kill someone."

"Perhaps he was working out his frustrations through his art."

I hold myself back from engaging in a debate on Taxidermy: Art vs. Craft and instead say, "Frustrations? He seemed to be a pretty satisfied dude."

"We all have our secrets."

"Why can't Grandma just chuck them in some Dumpster and call it a day?"

"He worked a lifetime on those things," Mom says. "They were his passion."

"Apart from the mademoiselles down at the bowling alley, you mean?"

"A little respect for the dead, Chrissy? I had the impression that when you were younger, you quite liked Grandpa. Before you hit your teen years and wrote us all off, that is. You're almost twenty now. Don't you think it's time you regained some civility?"

I roll my eyes, lean back in the seat, and think about the time right before Dad moved into his downtown condo with his first new girlfriend and Grandpa drove me down to Niagara to see the falls. The warplanes were buzzing atop my so-called-stable, dual-parent life, and there I was riding shotgun in a Lincoln Continental going one-fifty with a seventy-year-old man who was chain smoking Canadian Classics and holding forth on why the Premier of Ontario was essentially the left hand of Satan. It was the only full day I have ever spent in Grandpa's presence and was probably closer to the edge of things than any eight year old should ever get. Mom must have been in a pretty desperate state to let it happen.

Our car races through another intersection and I try to be subtle as I brace my hands against the seat.

"I don't want to fight with you right now," Mom says as she eases back slightly on the gas. "Let's just shut up and get this over with."

"Works for me."

Mom told me it burned her up how Grandma had been dressing in black and playing the grief card when the whole town knew she couldn't stand the sight of Grandpa while he was alive and that he'd screwed everything that moved within a hundred-mile radius. Again, that's not how she said it, but I'm never one for window dressing. Respect for the dead, clearly, is reserved for the sober.

Sometimes it's hard to reconcile my somewhat ranty but well-meaning Niagara Falls tour guide with the philandering man-demon of Mom's genesis legend. He was somewhat unimpressed with the lack of bravery I displayed in Dracula's Haunted Castle on Clifton Hill, but he hardly seemed to be someone worth telling a therapist about.

Grandpa even tried to help me, in his way, to make sense of all the bullshit that was about to come at me with respect to my parents. I didn't officially know about the divorce at the time, but I had more than an inclination. "Chrissy," he said as we strolled Falls-side, shirt cuffs coated in melted ice cream, "this is a shitpile of your father's making. It has zip to do with you. I'm not one to get down on a guy for running around, but here's the real problem: he never gave our Millie a moment of joy. Never pulled her out of herself, you know? A few of those good times can stretch a thin bridge over a lifetime of hogwash, but the complete absence of them? A human being just can't take that. Your grandmother feels differently, but I don't blame our girl for showing your dad the curb."

He then pulled a stuffed weasel, with its mouth agape and claws drawn, out of his rucksack. He told me I could keep it on my dresser so I could wake up every morning, look at it, and remember not to take anyone's shit. The man was a goddamn philosopher, really. I probably should have made some effort to visit him once I got a bit older, and set family feuds aside.

When we get to Grandma's apartment, she comes to the door in a getup reminiscent of Winona Ryder from *Beetlejuice*. Her heavy dress resembles an oversized reusable shopping bag, and her wide black hat frames her thinning hair like a halo of death.

"I'm surprised you came," she says.

I try not to stare at the way Grandma's eyeliner creeps down the fissures of her lower lids. Her eyes lock with mine and I feel her appraise me. Grandma hasn't seen me since well before my goth era began. I had missed Grandpa's funeral due to a nasty case of mononucleosis.

"Christine, I presume?" she says and backs away from the doorway so we can enter.

"She's going through a phase," Mom says as she brushes past a pile of open cardboard boxes in the hallway.

"Aren't we all?" says Grandma. She closes the door behind us.

In the foyer I am met by a portrait of my grandparents on their wedding day. Their formal dress and austere expressions give no hint that they are the same two folks who, if Grandpa was to be believed, would later find themselves halfway up the Humber River getting arrested for being drunk, disorderly, and trespassing on "some uptight asshole's farmland."

I look from the portrait to the unsmiling face of the woman before me and remember what Grandpa said to me while we had waited in line for the *Maid of the Mist*. "Your grandmother wasn't always religious. That part of things came before and after. There was a time when she would cut a rug with the rest of us. She was a goddamn tornado, but she blew herself over."

Mom and I sit on the mohair couch in the parlour. Grandma removes her hat and sits in a well-worn velvet chair opposite us. On the windowsill behind her are two fruit bats posed in mid-flight, their shiny wingtips splayed atop her greying hair. I cover my mouth and try not to think of an old *Kids in the Hall* sketch my cousin used to watch called "Hecubus's Pit of Ultimate Darkness." Grandma's eyes dart to my black-polished nails. I slide my fingers further down my thighs so she can get a better look.

After a long silence Mom says, "How are you doing, Mother?"

Grandma brings her thumb and index finger together and executes a subtle flick.

"As well as can be assumed."

"I'm never sure what to assume about you, Mother, which is why I asked."

"I wonder if you care, Millicent?"

Mom's face flushes and I can almost feel the pain in my own tongue from how hard Mom is biting hers.

"I've been alone twelve months," Grandma continues, "and I can count on one hand the number of times you've called."

"The phone works both ways, Mother," Mom says.

"But, of course, I am grieving my husband," says Grandma.

"We're both grieving, Mother. Your husband was, after all, also my father."

"Yes. You were always closer to him than you were to me, although I've never understood why. I always thought you and I had more in common."

"Can we just not?" Mom says, and I fail to suppress a snort as I realize she has stolen one of my best lines.

Grandma reaches behind the unsettling inanimate otter on her end table and chooses a cigarette from a low bronze dish.

"And how have you been keeping, Christine?" says Grandma as she flicks her lighter. "I hardly recognized you under all that makeup. It's a wonder your mother lets you leave the house looking so ghoulish."

The first exhalation of smoke does nothing to diminish Grandma's own low-grade demonic aspect.

"Touché, Grams."

Mom slides her hand to her chest and says, "Chrissy, please," but I see a fire light itself behind Grandma's eyes.

"I'm not sure I understand you, Christine," Grandma says.

"We are, all three of us, women of mystery," I reply.

"I see," Grandma says, "that you have become almost as uncivil as your mother. A shame, really. I remembered you to be such a gentle child."

Mom rises abruptly from the couch and crosses the room.

"Okay, let's go, Chrissy. This was a bad idea."

"Wait, what? We just got here. What about the zombie zoo? You can see she's already started to unpack them."

Grandma keeps her eyes fixed on mine as she addresses Mom.

"No, Millicent. Please stay. I insist, actually. I would like to understand what Christine is trying to say to me."

Mom picks her purse up from the floor and fishes for her keys.

"This is how it always goes," says Mom. "Five minutes and we're fighting."

"We're not fighting, Millicent. I am trying to have a conversation with Christine. You're always so sensitive. Just like your father."

"I guess that's why you can't stand me, then."

I flinch a little as Mom's hand creeps again toward her sternum.

"The world has always been a stage for you, Millicent," Grandma says.

Mom tugs her fingers through her hair and succeeds in ruining it. She stares at the ceiling, and I can tell she's trying not to cry.

The sight of her standing there on the edge of her little cliff is just too much, even for me. I slide into Mom's vacated seat and draw closer to Grandma.

"If you want to know, I was pointing out the irony of our similar appearances."

I sometimes go full professor when I'm getting mad.

"Go on," Grandma says, treating me to the full force of her glare.

"I think it's fair to say that we're riffing on the same aesthetic here. Black dress, black shoes, macabre makeup … "

"I have good reason for my appearance, Christine," Grandma says, and I feel my spirits rise because I realize I've got her goat. "I am in mourning for my husband."

"And I am in mourning for the innocence of my youth, Grams. We've all got our motivations. Besides, word on the street is you couldn't stand the sight of old Gramps."

Once I get going, I can become unstoppable.

"I simply cherished Carl, Christine, and you have no call to say that I didn't."

I guess Grandma likes to hit it with the 1940s church-lady lingo when *her* fur is up.

Mom goes to stand before the front door, and I notice her hand shaking as she unsuccessfully tries to turn the knob.

"Chrissy, please. Let's leave."

Grandma pivots her knees and turns sharply to Mom.

"Did I ever say I disliked your father, Millicent?"

Mom stares at the smooth surface of the front door and speaks so quietly I can barely hear her.

"You were always disappointed in him."

"You can easily love people who disappoint you," Grandma says.

A finely combed red fox stands in attack position at Mom's feet, and I think I can almost see a tear budding in its tiny, glazed eye. It seems we have the entered the telenovela zone of our conversation and I'm not ashamed to say that is where I usually hit my stride. I channel the badger that crouches on my bedside table and dive straight in.

"Okay, girls, gloves off and let's have at it," I say. "Old Gramps was a tomcat, which may have had something to do with Gran's winning attitude and sunny disposition, but fact is, Grams hated him for it. So she takes it out on young Millicent, who spends eighteen years drowning in a childhood pool of bitterness and then another nineteen years filling up a similar pool for me. Then the old coot goes and dies on us while we're all ignoring the hell out of him and now none of us knows what to do with all our shitty feelings. And so here we are ... on this afternoon of our discontent."

Both Mom and Grandma turn to face me, and I'm suddenly not sure what to do with all the attention in the room. Lucky, Grandma takes the mic.

"Are you quite finished, Christine? May I speak now?"

I get up from the couch and walk to the window to put some space between myself and the situation I've just conjured. That's the thing about me. I always seem to be sinking myself into shit swamps I can't wade my way out of.

"Yeah. Go ahead," I hiss, fingering the fuzz of some long-dead racoon's ear as my bravado deflates. Adrenalin, that bitch, always lets you down eventually.

"Your grandfather was a complicated person, Christine, as, I suspect, are you. But there are many reasons to mourn him, and so I do."

I turn to see that Mom has re-entered the parlour and is standing somewhat straighter than she had been when she was at the door.

"It is not for you," Grandma continues, "to judge how I go about mourning."

Mom flips her purse strap up over her shoulder and throws a look in my direction. "Yes, fine, Mother," she says, "but don't you think the black widow shtick is a bit much? I mean, it's not like you miss him."

102

Grandma folds her hands in her lap and tips her chin sideways.

"I am not a spider, Millicent. I am, as you well know, a religious person, and tradition dictates that a woman in mourning should wear black to honour the memory of her departed husband."

Mom rolls her eyes and kicks aside some of the crumpled packing paper from the empty taxidermy box at her feet.

I come to kneel in front of Grandma. When I grab Grandma's hand and bring it toward me, I can feel both her and Mom stiffen at the audacity of this intimate act. We are not, after all, a family of huggers.

I run my finger across the ebony ruffle of Grandma's sleeve and say, "Yeah. But maybe, underneath the shroud of the departed, you could wear a hot pink blouse. Nobody would have to know but you. And every so often you could let the cuff show, just a little, just to know you're still in there."

I feel Grandma's hand relax against me. When I look up into her eyes, I'm surprised to find them wet with tears.

"My God ... " says Grandma.

"I know ... " says Mom.

"She's his twin. He was never happier than when he was causing mischief."

The sound of Grandpa's laughter bubbles to the surface of my mind. I remember the rough texture of his fingers, how they smelled of cigarettes and gasoline. I remember him handing me a Cherry Garcia ice cream the size of two fists, and then leaning down to whisper in my ear, "As long as we eat it before we get home, Grandma will never know."

I can feel the mood turning sentimental and of all the mazes I've navigated in my nineteen years on this earth, sentimentality is never one I've been able to find my way through. My stomach starts to churn with the world around me, and I suddenly feel the need to exit the scene.

My rescue comes in the form of a whistling sound from the other room.

"Did you leave the kettle on, Mother?" Mom asks.

Grandma looks off in the direction of the kitchen and I'm surprised at how her voice sounds almost shy as she says, "I thought maybe we would have tea before we tended to the animals."

"I'll get it," I say, and I bolt from the room.

As I approach the kitchen, Grandma's old table comes into view. Polished chrome and melamine, a 1950s dream, it was the place where I'd sat with Grandpa when we got back from Niagara. I remember how I'd pushed the carrots across my plate, and the irritated way Grandma had said, "It's a wonder neither one of you are hungry, considering how long you were out."

An angry cloud of steam hurls itself across the window above the sink, and my mind takes me back to the bottom of the falls. Grandpa and I had pressed ourselves to the stern of the *Maid of the Mist*, two ants in blue plastic rain ponchos, packed tight with rest of the crowd as the ferry's motor screamed against the current of the mighty Niagara River. I remember the feeling of being suspended, engulfed in the boat's struggle to stand still in the water. I remember the rush of the waves as they crashed around us, how for a moment, the thin crust of the earth we existed on seemed to disappear beneath them. I remember the feel of Gramps' breath on my ear, how the smell of Jack from the "one last drink before we the road back to Hamilton" had lingered in the moist air.

"Look at that, Chrissy," he said. "That's Mother Nature showing you her whole ass."

For that moment I had forgotten about my parents, my troubles at school, all the bullshit that had been polluting my eight-year-old mind. I just watched the seagulls beat their wings, dive, and try to catch a moment where they could ride the slipstream before facing the roar.

"It's like the world could just swallow us if it wanted to," I'd said. And, when I think of it now, I wonder if that's when my goth phase really started to emerge. "Yeah," Gramps had said, "but she won't. Not just yet, Chrissy. She'll keep coming back for more as long as you deserve her."

I hear the sound of Mom and Grandma's footsteps behind me and watch as their images settle along the steamed surface of the glass.

"Did you know he filled me up with ice cream, so I'd be too full for supper that day he took me to the falls?" I ask.

"Of course I did," says Grandma. She rests her hand on the wall beside me. "He was an absolute devil till the day he died."

"Did it bother you, Grandma?" I ask.

"How could it not have?" she replies.

I stare through the condensation and into the reflection of the three of us huddled in the doorframe like a modern version of the opening scene of *Macbeth*.

"Bullshit it did," Mom says, and both Grandma and I turn to face her. "I was stuffed to the gills with Cherry Garcia every time he brought me back from our little adventures," Mom continues. "He told me you'd never catch us as long as I destroyed the evidence before we walked through the door."

"Which was incredibly inconsiderate of the effort I'd made – "

"You were always sour at us when we got back from the falls," Mom says. "But I saw how your expression changed in the reflection of the window when you turned back toward the sink."

"What do you mean, Mom?" I ask.

"She was always trying not to laugh," Mom says. "Didn't want to give him the satisfaction."

Grandma tries for a dour look, but her eyes betray her, and eventually she gives up the struggle and relaxes her face.

"He took me there for our honeymoon after we got out of jail," Grandma says, "and I'll always remember what he said on that little boat when we got to the bottom of the falls ... "

"Nature showing you her whole ass," we say in unison.

Grandma crosses to the counter and lays her hand atop a cardboard box that is still taped shut. "I found this when I started to sort through the back room," she says. "I thought, despite everything, that we should open it together."

On top of the box is a markered message written in Gramps' uneven scrawl: *For my girls.*

Grandma takes a knife from the counter and places it in Mom's hand.

"Here's hoping he means us," I say.

"Jesus, Chrissy," Mom says as she slices through the tape.

Inside the box is a taxidermy seagull. Unlike the rest of the animals in Gramps's menagerie, the bird is serene. Its feet rest firmly on a painted blue pedestal and its wings are slightly furled, as if the bird has just landed or is deciding to take flight.

Grandma reaches inside the box, pulls out three photographs, and hands one to each of us. In each photograph is a younger version of ourselves with Gramps, standing beside him in front of Dracula's Haunted Castle.

For a brief moment, before the three of us slip back into our respective roles, there is a ripple of connection that flows between us. We watch the current of accumulated steam as it trickles down to the windowpane and think of the Niagara River – how it feels to stand still, if just for a moment.

The Poacher

Jim Marchand is about to lose something that does not belong to him.

"Motherfucker," Doug hisses and smashes his paddle downward. He glides across the moonlit lake and an old Jack pine comes into view. Back in town, there is a map that marks this as the western edge of Marchand's property, but Doug has lived long enough in this bush to know ownership is fiction.

Doug remembers Marchand's self-impressed grin and the way he had slid his hand across Marianne's thigh when Doug had last seen them down at the co-op. Marianne herself had been unrecognizable, all dolled up and sounding like she had just walked off a talk show.

Back when they were an item, Marianne and Doug had spoken plainly and fought with cutthroat precision. That was one of the things Doug had always liked about Marianne. Nobody ever said she was a sweetheart, but you always knew where you stood. Doug has stayed up many nights thinking about Marchand and all his SUV pals down at the steakhouse, wondering why Marianne would go and make herself into such a fake just to impress a bunch of shitheads like them.

Doug raises his paddle from the water and rests it across the gunwale of the canoe. He closes his eyes and concentrates on his breath like the social worker taught him to do.

Doug, like Marianne, is descended from a long line of animals, but Children's Services let him live with his auntie for long enough to achieve a small base of inner calm. Marianne hadn't been so lucky. Sometimes her dad had taken her up to the water and held her face under as punishment for her back-talking, but even that mistreatment had failed to break her.

When Doug opens his eyes, he sees the current has eased him closer to his destination. The lights of Marchand's bush cabin twinkle through the trees.

Asshole's got enough cash to take her anywhere, but he brings her out here to hell's half acre? Nice friggin' honeymoon, pal.

Doug would have taken Marianne to Alaska like she wanted. She's been telling him since eleventh grade about the northern lights. He remembers lying with Marianne in back of his foster dad's flatbed, back when they were seventeen. They had been staring up into the clear autumn night and Marianne had said, "Word is those lights are like curtains of colour closing in over top of you. It'd be worth driving five thousand clicks to see something that magic. Even if it was only for a hot minute."

Doug takes his eyes from the lightless sky and eases the canoe aground beside Marchand's oversized Zodiac. He walks it backward and catches a whiff of his own sweat. He is pretty ripe, but a three-hour paddle doesn't leave most folks smelling too fresh. He could have trimmed it to forty minutes if he'd brought the skiff, but he knew keeping a low profile was key.

Doug follows the path upward from the shore and spots some prints in the moist earth. They're from Marianne's red runners, the shoes she'd kicked off beside a campfire two summers ago, right before she'd lowered her naked self down onto him.

Doug has been in love with Marianne for fifteen years. There is nothing in the world as real to him as her. The first time Doug saw Marianne they were both kids in care. He'd been wearing a Guns N' Roses concert tee, and she walked right up to him in her suede-tassel boots and said, "Axl Rose is ugly as shit and you look just like him, Bub." But then she'd laughed and continued: "If you can scream anywhere near as high as him, though, maybe I'll give you a try."

Right from the beginning, Marianne made Doug feel comfortable in ways that no one else could. She was rough enough to give him hell, to speak his language, but never cruel enough to inflict a wound he couldn't heal. She always kept Doug in the middle zone where he could breathe – not so sweet that he had to question her intentions, just sharp enough to let him know that she considered him a worthy adversary.

A snap beneath Doug's feet sends three bats fluttering from the woods. Doug stops, exhales, and tells himself to stay on target. He remembers Marianne's face in the flickering firelight on the night she cut him loose.

"I ain't gonna let you bully me," she'd said after he had asked her to marry him for the fourth time in a year. "Took me a lot to struggle out of my dad's trash pile. Not ready to dive back into the next one I see. Besides, your place don't even have running water."

Marianne had always been the planner between them. Doug had always been a right-now sort of guy. He should've thought more about who he was dealing with before backing her into that corner, but Marianne said it best herself: "Thing about you, Doug – you can only be who you are."

Doug lost hope when Marianne left him, and after he got out of the hospital, the doctor had set him up with the social worker. Doug is learning how to keep hold of his own reins now. He is ready to get things right.

Doug sticks to the shadows as he approaches the cabin. He passes the birch grove where Marchand punched him in the mouth last fall for felling a buck on his land. Doug remembers the feeling of his lip splitting beneath Marchand's unyielding fist. The social worker had suggested Doug was acting on a subconscious need to steal something back from Marchand when he'd poached the deer. Doug had initially called bullshit on her theory. He told her he had always been a hunter and had just been following the animal, but the more he thinks about it, the more he thinks the social worker was on to something.

Doug crouches low and conceals himself in the branches of a big birch at the edge of the yard. He squints past the porch light, and his heart lurches as he catches sight of Marianne. She runs her fingers through Marchand's hair and speaks in her nice-girl voice. Doug has only ever heard Marianne talk that way to her dad. Things must be worse than he'd anticipated. All she had said on the radio phone was, "Come tonight."

Marianne pours a whiskey straight from the bottle and places it in front of Marchand. Marchand tries to raise himself to drink it but then waves it away and returns his head to the porch boards with a thud.

Right on, girl. Always three steps ahead. Drunker he is, easier it'll be to shake him.

Doug gathers a few pebbles and tosses them up into the air. A bat swoops low to where they land, and although Marianne does not turn, Doug hears a slight pause in her monologue.

It's okay, Marianne. I'm here.

Doug waits in stillness for twenty minutes before Marianne eases herself from beneath Marchand's lax arm and creeps to the path's edge. Doug tries to touch the swollen edges of Marianne's lips when she gets close, but she raises her index finger between them. As they make their wordless way back to the canoe, Doug notices the hesitation in Marianne's gait and realizes the lip might be the least of her worries.

As Doug slips the canoe into the water, Marianne closes her eyes.

"Blow your breath out real slow," Doug whispers. "It'll help settle you."

Doug is surprised at how quickly Marianne complies but reminds himself of all the reasons she fears the water.

They are a few miles gone before Marianne speaks.

"Thought I could have it all, didn't I? Nice truck? Maybe a house and a couple vacations? Told myself he was a bit of a dick but he'd probably never clock me. And he didn't. Not till we got married. I'm dense, Dougie, but I'm not dumb enough to believe him when he says it won't happen again."

A spot of blood glistens on the edge of Marianne's lip. Doug wants to reach forward to wipe it but senses this is the wrong moment.

"Where should I take you, Marianne?"

Marianne opens her eyes just a crack, but it is enough for Doug to see the animal that still survives there inside her.

"Take me to your place, Dougie. But don't be expecting a thank-you screw. I don't owe you anything. And just so you know, you reek like rot."

Doug feels the weight of a year's worth of trouble lift from his shoulders.

"Be a cold day at Satan's beach house before I expect any appreciation from the likes of you, Marianne."

Marianne snorts, wipes the blood from her lip, and flicks it into the water with encouraging vigour.

Badly bruised. But not down for the count.

"Got the water hooked up now," Doug says.

"Must be my friggin' birthday," Marianne replies. She rolls her eyes as she recloses them.

Doug slips his paddle in the water and allows himself to hope.

We All Become Our Mothers

Georgie crushes her third cigarette of the morning against the inside edge of last night's shot glass. She sits at her vanity, slithers her hands across her silk-covered thighs, and flicks the light switch on her Hollywood mirror.

It's time to put on her face.

Georgie casts a glance at her reflection as she arranges her lipsticks and powders. A shrivelled old goat appears there, but Georgie doesn't pay her any mind. That sorry-looking beast will be gone soon enough; her sagging lines buried beneath a slick coat of Maybelline Dream #20 - Nude Beige.

Georgie is a blue eyeshadow type of gal. Her mother, Irene-Ann, never tired of telling her how blue was too young a colour for a woman past her prime, but Georgie didn't give two shits. She knew the sound of jealousy when she heard it trembling in her ears.

Georgie shakes open her bag of shadows: Shimmering Cobalt, Cerulean Chic, and Azure Sea. The pots scatter before her and Georgie's eyes fall upon the odd one out: Classic Pearl. Now there's a shade her mother would wear. Irene-Ann must have slipped it in there last year, sometime before she took her tumble down the cellar stairs. Georgie herself would never have purchased such a tired shade.

Georgie opens the pot and drags her finger through the white shadow. She presses the powder to her top lids, opens her eyes, and confronts the mirror. There, staring disapprovingly back at her, is a vision of Irene-Ann: same sunken cheeks, same pursed lips, same swollen nose.

"Georgina?" says the ivory-lidded ghost. "Just what have you done to yourself this time?"

Georgie leans back in her chair, lights herself another cigarette, and considers the macabre visage of her mother as it floats through the smoke. Georgie was a fool to think it could have been so easy to get rid of Irene-Ann. Not seven months in her grave and already the beast has gotten restless. Looks like she's decided to emerge, to creep her shrivelled mug straight out from under Georgie's own silky skin.

"I'll never forgive you for pushing me, you little Satan," says the ghost. She takes a long drag on her cigarette and blows the smoke out against the mirror. "Even though I know I goddamn deserved it."

Georgie brings herself in close to the reflection, looks Irene-Ann straight in the eye, and laughs. Georgie smiles her wicked smile, flicks the cigarette into the shot glass, and reaches for the Cerulean Chic.

"Haven't got me yet, you old bitch," she says.

The Witch's Tooth

My son, Lars, a snarl of sticky fingers and unbrushed seven-year-old hair, flies at me with his bloody mouth agape, and the first thing I think is, *Where is his sister?*

He slaps his hand into the middle of my blouse, looks up past my terrified eyes, and laughs. His sister, Ana, age ten, careens around the corner and announces, "His tooth is out!"

A torrent of possible explanations tumbles through my mind, and I say a silent prayer that, whatever the story, it does not expand beyond the confines of our backyard. A problem that involves the neighbours will put me to bed for the rest of the afternoon.

If worth were measured in diagnoses, our family would be the richest on our street. We sample from many chapters of the textbook that glares down at us from Dr. G's shelf during Lars's weekly appointments: ASD (Lars), ADHD/anxiety (me), agoraphobia (their dad – but no points awarded for him since he no longer lives here). It is only Ana who doesn't – yet – find herself pressed between the pages of that shelf-devil, and maybe that is why she is the Lars Whisperer and de facto leader of our household – despite her tender age.

Since Ana's birth and the abrupt arrival of my own adulthood, I have dreamed of living in relative tranquility, unfettered by the mutiny of life's circumstance or the inward rip of my own mind.

But crises stalk me like jilted lovers, so I am at once divorced, depressed, delayed, and excuse-me-universe-this-is-my-stop-and-I-would-like-to-get-off-now-please.

Lars peels his palm back from my blouse, and there – in the middle of the creeping stain – is his tooth, clinging to the material between my breasts by the jagged root. He eyes me with his peripheral vision as adrenaline buzzes through his small body, and he starts to flap his arms.

"Stop it," I say. "No flapping."

Ana gives me a look, and I can tell she is thinking of how Dr. G told us the flapping is just part of the syndrome, it's how Lars shows us he is excited, that we should embrace his differences, et cetera, et cetera. But whenever Lars starts to take flight, I remember my own ticks and twitches on the playgrounds of yore, the grief I endured at their expense, and I find myself wanting to spare him that dark nugget of childhood by the simple act of clipping his errant wings.

I think of Dr. G and how she reassures me Lars will "arrive to where he's going in his own good time." I get it; she's telling me to relax and not expect much from the nest of crossed wires that make up my son's brain. But whenever she says this, my eyes drift over to the silver frame on her desk containing a darling photograph of her three Miss Muffet daughters. I look back at her well-meaning smile and think, *How would she like, instead, to be the mother of the spider?* That is not to say there is anything *wrong* with the spider per se – and I love that spider, I do – but he is not the character in that story who makes the curds and whey an easy, relaxing dining experience.

Ana's commanding voice snaps me into the harsh light of the present, and, as always, she is three steps ahead. Her smile displays a crowded mouthful of adult teeth, proof of her undisputed expertise in all things dental, as she starts to rattle off the rules of the tooth fairy. Lars snatches his tooth from its precarious perch, bounds from the room, and the high siren of his displeasure sounds its receding alarm. "She can't have it, it's mine!" he says. I look askance at Ana, who rolls her eyes and gently informs me, "He's talking about the tooth fairy."

I follow the sound of Lars's ragged breath to the living room. The shaking leaves of our biggest houseplant bellow, "THAT-STU-PID-LADY-CANNOT-HAVE-MY-TOOTH-IT'S-MY-TOOTH-AND-SHE-DOESN'T-NEED-ANY-MORE-TEETH-FOR-HER-GREEDY-COLLECTION!"

Dr. G has stressed the importance of taking a breath before responding to Lars's outbursts, so I do this, but it does not really help and I still end up sounding like a rabid hyena. "But you will get two dollars! Think of all the candy!"

I'm not sure why this is the hill I have decided to die on. The last thing Lars needs is more sugar, but his rejection of the tooth fairy – one of the last remaining pillars of a normal childhood I feel capable of providing him – stings my heart. I wonder, like I always do, if we're wasting our time dragging Lars down to the clinic every Wednesday. No matter what we do, he seems to end each day the way he begins it: as far from neurotypical as he can possibly get.

Last week Dr. G told me to stick a dot in the middle of my forehead and get Lars to practice his eye contact by speaking directly to it. I am supposed to report how that went at today's session, but I forgot all about it until maybe an hour ago. In an attempt to compensate for my unforgivable neglect, I had asked Ana to draw an actual human eye on my forehead with lipstick and hoped its jazzy appearance would give Lars a much-needed shortcut to social success.

I sat Lars down at the table and Ana suggested he tell me the story of the horned deity and the moon goddess while trying to focus on the eye. I figured the story had something to do with the crystals growing in our windowsill, the mess Ana and Lars had recently made of the slow cooker, and Ana's casual comments about how she and Lars were "learning about earth magic." It was something I'd been meaning to pursue further but had lost track of – like everything else that is not directly linked to our immediate survival.

The lipstick eye had no real impact and Lars told most of his perplexing story to the wind chime behind my ear. Then he got so excited by what he was saying that he ran away flapping.

Kind of like what he's doing now, behind the dracaena.

Ana comes to stand beside me, lets out a long sigh, and says, "You have no choice, Lars, the fairy gets all of the teeth, and what are you going to do with it anyway?"

"NONE-OF-YOUR-BUSINESS!"

I open my mouth to scold Lars for his harsh tone – I mean, seriously, if Ana turns against him, I am not sure what we'll do – but Ana waves me away and approaches the plant.

"Lars, once a tooth falls out it's no longer part of your body … "

"UNTRUE!"

" … so you need to find a way to let it go."

"ANYONE-WHO-APPROACHES-ME-WILL-BE-ANNIHI-LATED."

I see the plant's pot edge closer to the end of its stand and I abruptly reach my limit for the whole frigging scene. I make a swipe at the trembling, waxy leaves of the dracaena. I feel Ana's small hand on my abdomen. She says, "Lars. It's time for a brain break."

Ana went to a group called Aspie Avengers for neurotypical siblings of kids with Lars's particular variety of autism. It is a watered-down version of Empowered Parenting, the group I was supposed to attend but left after the first hour because I could not pay attention and was too afraid the overconfident lady who was teaching it would ask me a question I couldn't answer.

The Aspie Avengers use all sorts of cool lingo – like "brain break" – which is supposed to mean zenning out and taking a breather, but to me it sounds like taking your brain and cracking it on the side of the counter.

Ana puts her arms out in a don't-even-think-about-it football stance, so I try to fake her out and go around but she knows my moves too well and blocks me. "Mom, Dr. G said physical restraint is the last resort."

Yeah. Right. And I guess Dr. G is going to come down here and clean up all the soil and blood that's about to hit the carpet? But what can I say? The kid is right. She's always right, and I should probably just accept that my own hysterical parenting is so rarely effective that it would be better if I just went the route of their dad, left them both the bank card, and skipped town altogether.

I start to pace between the fireplace and the sofa while Ana tries Lars from another angle. "If this situation was resolved, Lars, how would it look?" Goddamn, those Aspie Avengers are a slick bunch. There is a long silence as Lars considers this, and then the leaves of the dracaena grow still as he says, "My teeth would be all around my neck on a shiny piece of tinsel."

What can you say to that?

I wish I could clip a USB cable into Lars's ear canal and plug his brain in to the side of the television. I want to see on the screen whatever it is that scrolls through his mind. I want to indulge him, take him seriously, "explore the whole idea" and "make room for him to express himself" like Dr. G said. Tinsel? Teeth? Plural? Does he want to remove the rest of them? But Ana seems unbothered by the audacity of Lars's proposal and simply says, in her best Dr. G voice, "Tell me more."

Lars doesn't respond immediately, and I start to wonder if he will finally defeat his Whisperer, but then he walks out from behind the plant like he has just returned from a Sunday stroll and says, "I will collect all of them, make a necklace, and wear it to school."

I squeeze my eyes together and say a silent prayer for Ana's continued good health and cool head. I consider Lars, as he stands in our living room with his bloody smile and dancing eyes, and my mind conjures an image of him as a fifteen-year-old goth kid, clad in black, metal-faced, and morbid as hell. I see him wearing that necklace of his own teeth and telling the other adolescent wraiths it is no big deal. It is a thing of beauty, this vision of an adolescence so benign, and a hopeful sigh passes my lips.

Something presses hard on my big toe and I look down to see present-day Lars standing on the edges of my shoes. I can tell from the look on his face that he has just asked me a question, so look to Ana in desperation.

"He wants to know where he can keep it."

"What?"

"His tooth."

T minus twenty minutes to our appointment at the clinic but instead of disembarking the 11 Fairview bus in front of the hospital, we beat a path down Bath Street, on foot, toward the Occult Shop. It's true, what Ana said: where else would we find an appropriate vessel for collecting human teeth?

I hold the collar of Lars's coat in a death grip and he strains against me like an English setter who has spotted a river. Dr. G says it's natural to want to protect Lars, but I'm going to have to start giving him a little more freedom. I think she can say that because she's never witnessed him, with her own eyes, run headlong and laughing into traffic. She has also never had to deal with the Lululemon-Lexus Lady who caught hold of Lars last summer, just before he was almost crushed by a Bigman's Pizza truck, and then stood there considering if she should return Lars to his reckless life situation or throw him in the back of the Lexus and head straight to Children's Aid.

That afternoon represents a pretty low point in my life and I try not to remember it as much as possible, but the thing about my mind is it is a complete Judas, and, sometimes, when I'm trying to get to sleep, it presents me with the crushing memory of how I stood there on the street corner and sobbed to that fuchsia-clad temptress about how I'm a single mom of a special needs kid but sometimes I think there is more wrong with me than there is with him, and what I really need is someone to take care of *me*, and I had to ask her for a tissue because of course there were none in my pocket, and the Lexus lady looked at me with fake kindness that was really mostly boredom, and said, "Don't worry, you're a good mom," but she didn't mean it because how could she even know that when the only thing she knew about my parenting was that I'd let my son run into traffic?

Now Lars trips over his boot and slides into the side mirror of some one-percenter guy's parked Mercedes, and the guy yells, "Hey, why don't you fuckin' watch it?" and I yank Lars backward and say, "Hey, why don't you go suck a fuck?" so the guy looks up at me like he's ready to fight, and Lars starts singing, "SWEAR, SWEAR, SWEAR, SWEAR." Ana plants her hand in the small of my back to urge me forward, and the Mercedes guy makes the correct assessment that he has a lot more to lose in this than I do, so he puts his shiny beast in gear and drives off, shaking his head as Ana and I gallop ahead to catch Lars before he reaches the next intersection.

I pull out my cell and call the clinic. I tell them I have a family emergency, and I know they don't believe me because it is the third family emergency in as many months and I'm pretty sure they can hear the cacophony of Bath Street in the background, but that's the gold of a family emergency, you never have to provide details because it's private and unless they 're willing to call you out and risk hearing that you are, at the very moment they're accusing you of being a big fat liar, getting an abortion or watching your sister take her last breath, they cannot really do much except reserve some time during your next appointment to ask how you are coping and "assess for caregiver burnout."

I hang up with the clinic and it's onward to the witches.

I look at Ana and consider her face, illuminated by the afternoon sun. Her expression is relaxed but there's a hint of expectation nipping at the back edges of her gaze. Lars begins walking at a slower pace and I rest my open palm on his shoulder as we proceed south. His voice is pure Blue Zone with no trace of robot as he says, "Ana, do they have obsidian at the witch store?" Ana looks at him like he's just asked if they have ice cream at Baskin Robbins and says, "Uh. Huh. This is going to be awesome."

Somewhere in a dusty corridor of my brain, I hear the faint sound of a pin striking solid mush. I am usually the last person in this crew of bandits to figure out what's really going on, so it's no small wonder it has taken me this long to realize that the trip to the Occult Shop is not about Lars and his escaped tooth, it's about Ana and her newfound witchy dreams.

Now that my thoughts have stumbled on the right path, the evidence falls in front of me like gentle snow. I remember the surprise package from Amazon that arrived last week and the subsequent revelation that Ana had ordered an Introduction to Spells and Crystal Starter Kit online with my credit card. I remember how she explained to me, patiently and without a shred of remorse, that she had been planning for some months on "taking the next step toward Wicca," and when the crystal starter kit went on a forty-eight-hour sale there was just no time to consult me. I know I should be mad at her, but at the time it had seemed to all make sense. Ana has a way of saying things that I think might be an actual form of hypnotism, and sometimes I worry if this is how she is when she's twelve, is there any hope for me really? By the time she's fourteen I'll probably just live in a cocoon in our attic, and she'll come up once in a while, have me sign some papers, and then wiggle her fingers and whisper "It's okay, Mom, shhhhh ... shhhhh ... just go back to sleep.

"Mom! Red light!"

Lars slips his shoulder out from under my hand, and as I reach forward to recapture him, I see an old blind woman and her German shepherd standing patiently beside us, waiting for the light to change. I marvel at how perfectly her lipstick matches her sunglasses and wonder how she manages to do it, despite her obvious disability. She clacks her cane back and forth on the edge of the curb and I briefly consider how helpless she would be if the German shepherd got tired of his life of servitude and led her into the dark woods.

"Is it possible to attach your dog to a sled?"

The lady looks toward the sound of Lars's voice and says, "Beg your pardon, son?"

"Your dog has a harness similar to the husky dogs of the Arctic. I recently watched a YouTube program about the Inuit people of northern Quebec and their ability to affix their canine pets to large sleds and be pulled across Hudson Bay."

The lady laughs and says, "I never thought of it that way."

"You might consider it for winter travel."

"Wouldn't that be a sight, eh, son?"

Then they both laugh but for different reasons, and I can tell Lars does not know what to say next so he starts counting down the numbers as they flash on the perpendicular side of the intersection. "Four, three, two, one, hand. Now we can proceed." The lady's fingers hover like hesitant moths over Lars's head and then land gently atop his wind-blown hair. "Thanks for your help, son."

I realize she thinks he was counting for her so she would know when to cross the street, and I open my mouth to correct her. I want to tell her Lars has probably not pieced together she is blind and he looks for things to count when he is feeling lost or nervous, but before I can say anything, Lars looks up at the lady's bejewelled shades, simply says, "You're welcome," and follows her across the street.

Ana urges me forward and as I proceed, the foreboding black sign of the Occult Shop creeps into view. I have always been aware of the shop in the same way I'm aware of someone on the subway with a medical condition or a weird tattoo: I always want to look longer but don't feel I can deal with the social consequences of that commitment.

There is a pentagram carved on the door's face and I hesitate before it. As far as I know, it's the actual sign of the devil and maybe there are limits to my bad parenting, but Ana informs me it is only Satanic if it is upside down with a goat head in the middle, so I gather my strength and push open the door.

Inside, the shop is filled with waxy air that reminds me of elevators in the '80s, back before everyone got into scent-free and no smoking.

We turn toward the counter and there sits a morbid-looking youth who is a vision of Billy Corgan from the Smashing Pumpkins – not middle-aged, experimental stuff Billy, but melancholy Billy – that pale idol of my high school desires who foxed me with his smoky eyes and told me the world was a vampire.

The youth sits perched in front of a shelf of jars brimming with mysterious powders and unburned incense. His hair hangs heavy, a cascade of volcanic black, over his hollow cheeks. His feet are planted beside him atop a high stool and he leans his head forward between his pointed knees. His mouth twitches into a smirk: mysterious, unreadable, as if at this very moment, beneath his delicate lips, two vampire's teeth were easing their way through his glistening gums.

A low giggle bubbles from the base of Lars's throat and he begins to bob like a buoy on a rough sea. I survey the room and am somewhat alarmed to find the shop empty of customers, meaning we will have this Billy creature's undivided attention for the duration of our shopping experience. I'm not sure I can withstand the scrutiny of his full, unblinking gaze, so I'm somewhat relieved by the ordinary way he says, "Can I help you?"

Ana is all business. She approaches the counter and says, "We need a vessel for teeth."

"Human or animal?"

Ana fixes Billy with a haughty stare that says, *What do you take me for, bud, a part-time witch?* She says, "Human," and slaps Lars's tiny tooth on the onyx counter. I guess that is when shit gets real for Billy because he pauses briefly (for effect?) and says, "I guess I'll have to get Ariel from downstairs."

Billy looks toward an ancient-looking wooden door behind him and presses a green button underneath the counter. The muffled sound of a chime rises through the floorboards and is followed by a rustle, like some beast has been awakened from a long sleep. As footsteps ascend the creaking staircase, I feel Lars shift behind me and exhale in short bursts.

Billy considers the door with an air of great expectation, and we all hold our collective breath as the handle begins to turn. The door eases open and there appears an earthly vision of Athena with brown, matted locks streaming from her scalp and coming to rest atop her broad shoulders. Her black fishnet top struggles valiantly to contain her solid arms, which are coated from armpit to fingertip with coloured tattoos of symbols whose meaning I can only imagine.

Ana touches my waist and she whispers Ariel's name like a tentative wish. Her head comes to rest solidly in the crook of my arm and I realize it has been an eternity since my daughter has sought solace in my embrace, and I pause to marvel at the brief return of what I hadn't known was missing.

Billy's splendour is greatly diminished beside Ariel's luminous glow, and as he steps behind her to close the wooden door he says, "Ariel is the owner," as if he is announcing a titled lord. Before I have a chance to construct a fully formed thought, I blurt out, "Isn't that the cat from the Smurfs?" and Ariel's face goes dark while Billy takes a step backward and hisses, "That's Azrael."

But deities are often benevolent, and despite my offense, Ariel's eyes soften and she stares at me intently as if I am a strange piece of art whose meaning she is just coming to understand. "How can I help?" she says, as if the possibilities are endless.

"Well, my son's tooth fell out today, and apparently he takes exception to the whole concept of the tooth fairy and it's nothing against fairies — don't get me wrong, he's usually very interested in magic, and in fact, my daughter is thinking of becoming a witch herself, not that witchcraft is magic, but you know what I mean —

anyway, he needs a pot, or possibly a miniature cauldron, or something to put his teeth in as they start to fall out, because he wants to make a necklace … "

Mercifully, Ariel raises her finger and says, "Show me the tooth." I look down at the counter and realize with the sickening certainty of a sudden car crash that the tooth is missing.

I slam my open palms on the counter and my brain buzzes with panic. Lars unravelling behind the dracaena is one thing, but a meltdown among actual witches is stepping up to the plate for a whole new ballgame of danger and uncertainty. As I creep my hands across the unforgiving black Formica counter, I find myself longing for my former life of this morning, where the biggest dragons I had to slay were my mortal neighbours Ron and Sheila and their occasional petulant calls to the city.

A sound like the beating wings of a dragonfly commences behind me and I don't need to turn around to know it is Lars starting to fidget. The frequency of his vibration increases with the rate of my own heart as I press my chin to the smooth edge of the counter, cast my eyes sideways across its surface, and tell myself if I view things from a different angle, the tooth will materialize. I think about Lars and his flapping arms and how his tooth is only one of the many things he is missing, and I wonder how he is ever going to make it in a world where terrible occurrences like this one lurk around every goddamn corner.

Billy crouches down behind the counter and I feel the tingle of his stare across my scalp. His expression is quizzical and his warm, milky breath creeps across the counter's surface as he says, "Can I ask what that is on your forehead?"

Oh God. The lipstick eye.

My chin remains firmly stuck to the counter as I snap my (functional) eyes up to meet Billy's intrigued gaze. Ariel drags her ebony fingernail across the keys of the cash register and slowly exhales.

And so, here it is, the moment where I just give up.

I long for a smoke bomb to throw down on the floor so I can spew forth an impressive screech and disappear into the netherworld, but I know there is no real chance of such an impressive yet tidy exit, and my heart starts to hammer in my molars as I come to realize it is not only Lars who might have a meltdown here in the dwindling afternoon of the Occult Shop. But help can come from the strangest places when you are knee-deep in a time of need. Ariel's voice booms out from behind the counter. "It's the eye of Horus, you ass, she's obviously in need of protection."

I look up at Ariel, with her monstrous forearms and billowing hair, and I wish she would just throw me over her netted shoulder, carry me down into her basement, and rock me to sleep. But instead, she slides a crystal made of blue translucent columns across the counter until its miniature peaks brush my fingertips. "Blue kyanite," she says as she looks straight through to the back of my skull. I hear Ana behind me whisper, "It drives away anger, confusion, and stress, and inspires a capacity for linear and logical thought."

Ariel beams down at Ana like she is a freshly combed Persian kitten. I feel Ana return to a safe zone behind my back and realize that despite her bravado and appetite for credit card fraud, Ana is not ready to face down an actual witch.

A moment of stillness falls on the Occult Shop. My fingers tingle with blue kyanite and I wonder if it can really be this simple? Can we all just live a normal, restful life? One without screaming houseplants, bloody shirts, or the brutish requirements of well-meaning women with PhDs?

I feel a white energy surround me, and a thousand mouths sing with voices I cannot hear with my actual ears but rather feel as the vibrating rays of my own being. A smell tickles the edge of my nostrils; it is a sweet smell, something like lavender mixed with Morning Dew dishwasher detergent. I inhale deeply of the mythical air that surrounds me, and I know Ariel can smell it too because she turns her head gently toward it.

Billy draws his own deep breath, and then he, the living avatar of my teenage dreams, gives me a long look and says, "Ma'am, do you know where your son went?"

My heart lands hard on the unyielding floor and spatters its invisible blood all over my shoes.

The clicking behind me becomes more insistent and now it sounds less like an angry dragonfly and more like the strike of a cheap lighter. I hear the low growl that Lars makes when he is just about to execute an incredibly interesting yet destructive plan, and I turn on my heel to make a hasty survey of the shop, but, of course, he is nowhere to be seen.

I sprint past a glass case filled with shimmering pyramids, enter a narrow aisle lined with incense, and shriek Lars's name as if he is five miles inside a dark cave and I am at its mouth. Lars doesn't answer my call, but there is no need because before me is a large circle, drawn on the floor in an uneven arc of sand, and in its centre stands Lars.

Four lit candles of red, blue, yellow, and green divide the circle into four quadrants, and at its far edge lies a brass bowl atop the crumpled heap of Lars's shirt. A thin stream of smoke drifts skyward from the bowl and the smell of turkey stuffing combines with the soapy mélange.

As I draw closer to the circle, I see Lars's tooth resting on a smooth black stone that has been precisely placed on a bed of sticks inside the bowl.

Ariel's voice takes on an otherworldly dimension and she turns to Billy and says, "He's made a circle." Billy's eyes go wide, he presses his palms together in sudden prayer, and says, "Pennyroyal, sage, and obsidian."

Ana's thumb slides up my spine, and she whispers, "A protection spell, we read about it in the book from Amazon." Ariel and Billy nod and their eyes remain firmly fixed on Lars, who paces the circle and recites some words I cannot understand. Ana's voice sounds hesitant and small as she asks, "Mom, do you think

Lars is a real witch?" and my brain screams, *No-no-no-no he's just a kid who's great at memorizing stuff and he doesn't need another god-damn label!* But then Ariel and Billy say, "Oh yeah. Definitely," in unison.

Lars stands shirtless with his back to us and starts to sway to some unheard tune. I think of the early years of The Doors and how Jim Morrison would stand with his back to the crowd, paralyzed with stage fright, and count down the seconds until he whipped around and slayed the crowd with his tiger's growl and freaky moves.

From the corner of my eye, I see Ariel and Billy start to groove to Lars's rhythm, and I get the distinct impression that the storm of the friggin' century is about to rip through town. I am out of my depth, so I turn to Ana for guidance, but find that she has backed herself up behind the incense display and suddenly looks less like the wizened leader of our family and more like an actual twelve-year-old kid who just found out her brother is more than she bargained for.

Lars begins to pace the circle, and when he reaches the point closest to where I'm standing, he pauses as if he is waiting for something to happen. I take a hard swallow and try to fight against the screaming blank of my mind, but all I can think of is how if I had nothing to offer Lars when he was just a regular kid with autism, there is literally no way I'll be able to guide him through life if he's going to turn himself into a card-carrying wizard.

Between Lars and I is a small break in the crooked line of sand, and I realize what I must do. I step gingerly over the threshold between the earthly and magical dimensions. Lars takes some sand from his pocket and closes us inside the circle.

He looks straight at my lipstick eye and then raises his arms like an eagle that's about to take flight. He starts to hum, flap, and stomp his feet, and I'm not sure what to make of it, but then I become filled with a strange sort of heat that is somewhere between being stoned and having an asthma attack.

I take Lars's hands in mine, and he looks straight at me – not past me or near me, but pupil to pupil in a locked, spectral gaze. We start to move our hands together, and as we undulate around the inside of the circle, I feel it might be possible for our feet to leave the earth, that maybe me and my amazing son might rocket, hand in hand, up through the afternoon sky.

I look to Ana as her brain tries to navigate the moving parts of the circle. I sense her confusion, her fear that something seismic has busted beneath us, and I realize there are parts of her heart that beat with my own. I smile at her as Lars and I spin in the flapping wings of our human tornado, and then the sound of Ana's laughter cuts through the haze of everything around us. She takes her place on the perimeter of the circle and raises her arms high.

I let go of Lars's flailing arms and he glides like a sparrow over a misty pond. He looks back and flashes me his newly toothless grin. I stare into the dark space where his new tooth will grow and consider a truth whose crystal has just formed in my jittery mind.

Beneath the Pond

My eyes are closed but I am not asleep.

Nana and I are out by the pond because Grandpa has drinking to do, and it's best if we leave him to it.

I listen to the soft quack of the lady mallard as she cruises with her ducklings across the water.

She will only come close if I lie very still.

Ducks are careful creatures.

Nana and I spend most of our days out here among the wildflowers and pond creatures. We record their comings and goings in our notebooks, like scientists.

The lady mallard is our plain-Jane sweetheart. She's not as pretty as her drake, who sparkles in his green-jewelled crown at the far edge of the water. He doesn't care about the ducklings once they're hatched, and it's probably just as well. The lady mallard has it all under control.

I ease my eyes open to see her.

Her feet beat desperately underwater, but her body glides like a skate across the surface of the pond.

Nana's chest rattles against my scalp as she sleeps. In the night, Grandpa hollers that she sounds like a goddamn buzz saw, but I love to listen to her gentle vibrations.

Something rustles in the grass behind me. It could be the wind, but maybe it's something better.

The notebook lies beside me, open to the page that says *water-fowl* in Nana's tidy printing. I reach out my hand and silently flip to *other mammals*.

I listen to the blades shiver and wish for a rabbit, or maybe a white-tailed deer.

The grass goes silent.

The lady mallard quacks a warning to her ducklings as she swims in a circle at the edge of the pond. She is closer to me than she has ever been.

Nana snores on as I redirect my creeping hand toward the water. I am forbidden to touch the animals, but I long to feel the slick surface of the lady mallard's back on my fingertips, just this once.

The sound behind me starts again, but I ignore it. The chicks have scattered into the cattails but the lady mallard waits for me. Her webbed foot pounds beneath the surface of the pond like a flashing yellow light.

I hover my hand on the edge of her tail feathers and something tight grips my leg.

I smell Grandpa's drinky breath as he says, "Go on, Sonja, snatch her up."

I turn my head and see him, stretched out on the grass behind us, his hand wrapped around my ankle. His eyes are red and watery, but they shake with excitement. I look toward Nana and hesitate.

"Don't worry about her," he says smoothly, "she can't keep her finger in every pie."

I feel the ripple of Grandpa's mischief and it makes me brave.

The lady mallard flaps her wings and makes a colossal racket. I dive my hands into the water and scoop her out by the belly.

She is heavier than I expect.

I pull her upward and something comes with her. An old snapper, with his jaw shut tightly around the lady mallard's ruined leg, dangles there like the pendulum on an old clock.

Drops of red hit the surface of the water, and the turtle turns his trembling emerald eye toward me.

I drop the duck back into the pond with a splash and take a step backward.

Nana struggles to her feet as Grandpa snorts and giggles. He claps his hands twice and says, "Hungry little bugger. He got her good."

Nana grabs my shoulders and turns me sharply toward the house. We march like soldiers from the pond and Grandpa calls after us, "Come on, girls. It's the way of nature!"

Nana's strong hands push me forward as she whispers, "Leave him, just leave him."

The green grass shakes with Grandpa's laughter as the duck slips under the water.

Bone Jacked

Have you come to boogie, baby?

The janitor stands alone on the dance floor. He sways in the orbit of its still moon. Tiny diamonds hover but don't give chase as he sweeps forward remnants of torn tassels and lipstick-kissed cigarettes.

What's that look I see in your eye?

He points a steel toe and slides it across the vinyl tiles that simmer in the embers of the trembling light. The exit sign flickers as the street's breeze eases a breath of glitter across the room. The janitor extends his fingers and closes them over his outstretched palm. He strikes a pose.

Yeah, that's right, daddy. Get down.

The stars blur around him as they stretch thin the decades. A needle drops, a turntable starts, and the janitor begins to spin.

Explode with me, into hyperspace.

He is ensorcelled by visions of his dynamite baby as she boogies with the wings of heaven on her shoes. Her arms like melamine, unbruised and unbitten, weave like ribbons through the electric air.

You feel that, sugar, you feel it coming?

She beckons him with serpentine hips as he sways toward her; an errant curtain, caught in the torrent of her unexpected gust. He feels the wisps of her pull him tight, his vixen of velour, his panther of the pickerel print platforms, this ghostly vision of his years-gone love and its undoing.

You dance, you shake, you hurt.

His fingers descend the smooth shaft of his broomstick as he casts his line to reel her in. She vibrates on the wire, twirls inward, a needle through his soft flesh.

Gimme some skin, brother. That's right. That's right.

He leans the broomstick long against his locked knee as he invites his sweet apparition to toboggan the slope of his velveteen thigh. She ascends the gorge of his sequined neckline, and he whispers a prayer onto her creme-rinsed hair.

Stayin alive.

His dynamite baby's limbs scissor sideways as the janitor lifts her skyward. Together they rocket through the celestial blur; past the tendrils of her terrible tomorrows, the heartaches, the hospitals, the potions, the pills, the cluster of cables that failed to restart her heart of glass.

Say your prayers, baby, just don't care.

He launches her forward into the feverish night, propels her past the motionless moon, and watches as her body writhes toward the surface of the sun. Then his dynamite baby starts to sizzle as the needle slips its groove and the record stops.

Burn baby burn.

The broomstick clatters from the janitor's hands and comes to rest atop the pile of midnight leavings. The grit of the floor penetrates the thin layer of his brown corduroy knees and his ragged breath spreads across the ruffled cinders of the disco.

Catch you on the flip side, sunshine.

Baby, turn me loose.

All the Old Tricks

Carol shows us how to yank the leash so the dog will know we mean business. "If you want him to respect you," she says, "you will need a firm hand."

"Doesn't that hurt his neck?" asks Judy, the most vocal of the five dog owners in our semicircle.

"Nonsense," says Carol. "The dog is a hearty animal."

Judy has already asked too many questions.

Carol's lipstick bleeds down the front of her teeth as she hisses, "Heel." Mom glances at Carol's mouth and mumbles, "God, she's awful."

"We can leave if you want," I say. "Dad is already here."

Carol glares and her lips close like a pulled purse string. Our mastiff, Sammy, strains the leash and Carol sighs. The origin of Sammy's bad behaviour has become clear.

"No," says Mom as she runs her tongue over her own incisors. "He's a city dog now, he needs to be trained."

Mom looks out across the dry grass of the soccer field to where Dad sits, halfway up the bleachers. He peels back pink sheets of cotton candy from a cardboard stick and folds them happily into his mouth. Mom snorts. It has only been a year since the divorce, and she does not get over things easily.

"He's getting fatter by the minute," says Mom. "If he keeps that up, he'll be the size of a house."

Mom pivots and turns her back to Dad as she combs her fingers through her loose hair. Although she has tried to cover the scrape with makeup, I can see where her cheek hasn't fully healed from when Sammy bolted and dragged her halfway across the sidewalk.

"Dad's just here because he knows I can't stand the sight of him," Mom says.

"He's here because it's Friday and we're going to the farm."

"Friday starts at five o'clock."

I do not tell her it is ten past five.

I look back at Dad as he unravels another coil of pink fluff and winds it back around his index finger. Sammy leans hard on the leash and quietly whines. Carol appraises Sammy with raised eyebrows and shoots a look to Mom as if to say, *You know what you need to do.* Mom pulls the leash, but she doesn't have enough gusto to execute a Carol-style snap.

"Take control, Donna," says Carol.

Mom pulls harder and Sammy's breath gets ragged. "Stop it," I say. "Can't you see you're hurting him?" Mom lets go and Sammy's breath returns to normal. "Why can't he just live up at our old house with Dad?" I whisper. "He could run around the horse tracks with Grandma's dogs, and he wouldn't have to go to these stupid lessons and get neck-choked by you and crazy Carol."

Mom turns her head back to the bleachers and says, "And his bloody mother can feed him peach tarts and table scraps and he can run as wild as he wants to without a goddamn care."

"Exactly," I mutter.

"Wouldn't we all like to live like that?" says Mom. "Hanging out by the pond with Ingrid Fucking Danielsen while our wives are out working, never once worrying who we're dragging through the mud in the process?"

"Excuse me," says Judy as her dog starts to run circles around Sammy. "Would you mind watching your language?"

Mom stares unblinking at Judy until Judy's will crumbles, and then she turns her attention back to Carol. Carol calls for Sammy to come to the pitch and Mom hands me the leash. There is a hard edge to Mom's voice when she says, "Why don't you give him a try, Jamie? See if you have any better luck."

I take the leash and Sammy realizes in an instant who is at the reins. He lunges forward and I fall to the grass. The sky starts to spin around me, but I'm afraid to let go. The last time we lost Sammy, he was gone for days.

"Pull back on the leash!" hollers Carol as Sammy heaves me across the field.

I hear Mom's feet pounding behind me. "Let go!" she yells. "Jamie, let him go!"

I jerk back with all my strength on Sammy's leash, and he lets out a startled yelp. Sammy stands still in the field, choking on his own breath, and stares up at me with confused eyes. Carol approaches us and puts a hand on my shoulder. "That's the way, son," she says.

Mom's face is hard to read.

We all turn to see Dad laughing and ambling toward us. His arms are wide open to receive Sammy, whose entire body shakes with the momentum of his tail.

Mom helps me from the grass as Sammy springs free. Her eyes dart over all my surfaces and she pats me down, whispering "Okay, okay, okay." I jerk myself free of her and jog out toward the bleachers, released at last into the freedom of my upcoming weekend.

Sammy licks the sugar from Dad's lips as Dad draws him close. Sammy leaps forward, pushes Dad flat on the grass, and smothers him. Dad's mirth gathers force as he wheezes, "Okay, pal, love you too. Love you too."

A silence grows behind me and I turn to see Mom, alone now in the distant field. I stop short, unsure of how to proceed. She looks lost as she smooths her hair back from her cheek and takes in the chaos of dog kisses on the grass. I wave to her, but she doesn't see me. She stares at Dad and presses her hand to the side of her face like she is trying to hold something in place.

Unidentified Male

On his first night as a police officer, Amos Brownlea attends the scene of a homicide. The detectives circle in their trench coats as the ambulance lights reflect a staccato pattern across the street's silent puddles. The siren has quieted. The emergency is over.

Amos is the new guy, so he guards the body. The deceased, formerly tall, has become long. Amos is six foot four, big like his dad was. He sizes up the competition. Six foot three, maybe? Hard to tell because the guy's legs are a bit crooked. The voice of Amos's mother, Eunice, creeps into his mind. "Don't look at the body," she says. "It's a goddamn rookie mistake."

Amos squints into the darkness beyond the yellow tape and is relieved to see the news crew has not yet arrived. Once they set up shop, Eunice will be able to watch him on KPX-24's crime scene live feed. Amos needs to keep it together.

The thing Amos hadn't expected was the smell. It is subtle, a delicate mixture of sweat, sewer, and raw steak. Amos tries not to focus on it, tells himself he can get used to anything if he sticks with it, but the smell surrounds him like a twilight fog. Amos fears that if the mist were to clear, all that would remain would be an image of his dad. "That man is gone from this earth," says Eunice's voice, "and gone from our thoughts." Amos hops his attention to the next landing spot in his mind, avoids the dark hole between thoughts that threatens to draw him inside it.

The body is face down and clothed in a parka. When Amos's eyes drift downward, they fall on a red slick congealing on the furry edges of the parka's hood. Amos scans the sidewalk for someplace else to rest his gaze, and that's when he notices the blob of brain matter.

The blob resembles a dollop of clotted cream where it lies atop the frosted concrete. Although Amos looks at the blob directly, he does not really see it. He feels as if he is at home with his wife, Lola, watching a movie about a cop named Amos, and this is the scene where Amos stares blankly at a small piece of brain matter on the sidewalk and wonders what happened to all its thoughts.

Amos runs his finger along the inner seam of his pocket, finds Lola's paper, and eases it free. The paper says *Cops are hot!* in Lola's wavy script, and beside the letters, Lola has drawn a red set of lips. Amos brings the note to his nose and inhales the scent of Lola's strawberry pen. He does not think of his dad. He does not think of the phone calls or the quiet voices from the summer of 1998.

A paramedic asks Amos to help him spread an orange sheet across the body, so Amos jams the note back into his pocket.

"Get him covered up before the press comes, right, buddy?" the paramedic says. "Another five minutes and we'll all be the stars of late-night television."

Amos admires the paramedic's easy confidence and wishes he could share it. The paramedic's eyes scan the body as if it is simply part of the sidewalk. Amos wonders if he should kick the brain blob under the orange sheet but senses this is the wrong question to ask. Instead, he asks a different one: "Do we know who he is?"

"Unidentified," the paramedic says. "But we'll know soon enough. Lots of witnesses around when he was shot. Once word gets out to the family, we'll hear about it."

The sheet does not cover the body completely, so the deceased's feet and ankles remain in view.

"Tall drink, eh?" the paramedic says.

"Six three, I figure," Amos replies.

The paramedic's eyes bounce from Amos's steel toes to the top of his navy toque. "Guess you would know, buddy," he says.

A figure breaks away from the circle of trench coats to walk toward them. Amos realizes, from the scent of lavender and rose preceding her arrival, that the figure is Sergeant Tran. Eunice's voice whispers again in Amos's mind: "That woman stinks worse than a whorehouse bathroom."

A set of headlights crests the distant rise of Queen Street, and the KPX-24 news van comes into view. "Fucking parasites," says Sergeant Tran. "They'll be with us now till morning."

"Who the hell would want to waste their life watching twenty-four-seven coverage of us guys hanging around on the sidewalk?" muses the paramedic. Amos knows who. He thinks of Eunice.

Amos catches himself looking at the orange sheet again. The paramedic says, "A penny for your thoughts, buddy?"

Amos opens his mouth to tell the paramedic that the actual experience of attending a death is nothing like the photographs from his textbook, that being here with the sounds, the smells, and the real-time feelings has made everything much more sinister than he'd expected it to be, but luckily, before he finds his voice, Amos realizes the paramedic is making a joke. The paramedic crouches and hovers a copper coin in front of the blob on the sidewalk. Sergeant Tran rolls her eyes and a look passes between all three of them. They are a pack of tough dogs who can handle things.

Sergeant Tran squeezes Amos's shoulder and says, "There will come a day, Brownlea, when none of this will even touch you."

Amos considers the KPX-24 news crew as they unload the gear.

"How's your mom doing, Brownlea?" Sergeant Tran asks, and Amos stiffens.

"Donna Tran is the biggest hunk of dog shit the 36 Division has ever seen," Eunice's voice whispers through Amos's mind. Sergeant

Tran had been the one to finally report Eunice's drinking, forcing Amos's mother into retirement.

Amos answers with a snort and watches a cameraperson as he snaps the legs of a tripod into place.

Sergeant Tran grabs Amos's elbow and eases him away from the paramedic.

"I want you to know I'm someone you can talk to," she says in a low voice. "I realize I'm not your mom's favourite person, but I do understand the situation and I'm not unsympathetic. Especially when it comes to your dad and how that might affect you."

"I don't think about him ever," Amos says as he reaches under his toque, grabs a handful of hair at the nape of his neck, and squeezes hard. Sergeant Tran's eyes follow his action. Amos drops his hands to his pockets.

"You'll be fine, Brownlea," says Sergeant Tran. "Just fine."

As Sergeant Tran makes her way back to the group of detectives, Amos realizes she has been able to see through him, that her eyes have travelled past his new badge, through his bulletproof vest, and peered straight into the churning muck of his insides. Amos makes a mental note to bury things deeper.

Amos looks back to the sidewalk, to the blob, and forces himself to consider it. He tells himself that if he stares at the blob for long enough, it will become part of the sidewalk, like a pebble, like nothing. But this is not what happens. Instead, the blob seems to grow as Amos beholds it. He takes a step backward and realizes some part of him is afraid the blob will slither forth to touch the edge of his boot, perhaps crawl up his pant leg and start to ascend.

Amos texts his partner that he needs a piss break, so his partner comes out of the forensics van to stand beside the body. Amos heads over to the van, vomits quietly in the toilet, and flushes it down. He does not think of his dad.

Before the end of his shift, Amos sees two more bodies. One is a subway jumper, and Amos receives a high-five from the coroner when he locates the hand. The other is a "decomp case" – a body discovered by smell. Amos does not have to guard the decomp body. He just closes the apartment door and waits in the hallway for the removal crew to arrive.

After his shift, Amos takes a shower at 36 Division, but he cannot seem to remove the smell of the decomp from his skin. As Amos rubs himself red, another officer tells him the smell is probably lodged in his nose hairs. Amos raises his face to the shower head and chokes on the water. The officer laughs, so Amos does too. "Three corpses on your first shift, buddy," says the officer, "that's gotta be some sort of record."

"Soon, none of this will even touch me," Amos replies.

Amos rides the subway home and tries to distract himself with thoughts of Lola. Lola is a 1940s movie buff. She likes to watch the noir stuff – all those hard-jawed men with their .38 specials, leaning long on the mantle as they talk down their victory girls from the precarious edge of hysteria. After seven years of watching movies with Lola, Amos can do a pretty good Sam Spade impression. Sometimes he puts on "the voice," leans in close to Lola, and says, "Suppose you tell me about it from the beginning, doll?" Lola usually just rolls her eyes, but occasionally she lays her hand on Amos's thigh, and, if he's lucky, puts on her Mary Astor face and says something like "I've been bad, Sam, worse than you could know."

Usually, thoughts of fooling around with Lola distract Amos from the things that bother him, but this time it doesn't seem to work. The woman in the seat beside him rolls up her sleeve, and Amos imagines what her arm would look like disappearing beneath an orange sheet. As he examines the details of the woman's skin, Amos thinks of the detectives. He wonders how it would feel to be a modern-day Sam Spade. He remembers the firm pressure of Sergeant Tran's thumb on his bicep and the certainty in her voice as she had spoken to him. "Soon, none of this will even touch you," says the cool voice of Spade in Amos's mind, and he wonders if, when Tran had delivered that line in last night's film, he'd been playing the role of Mary Astor.

The woman beside Amos gets up and switches seats. Amos looks at his hands and finds them trembling. A wave of newly familiar nausea rises in Amos's throat, and he looks to the window. "Always look to the horizon, son," says Amos's dad's voice. "Let it steady you until the feeling passes." Amos can usually go whole months without thinking about his dad, so this new focus is unsettling. Amos counts the passing cars to force his thoughts onto a new path.

When the nausea fades, Amos looks to the faces of his fellow transit riders. He notices how their lips move, how frequently they blink, and how, when they speak, the sounds of their voices ebb and flow like a steady stream of ocean waves. He appreciates how they are all so animated, so present, so alive.

Amos is happy for the people of the subway, glad for their simple existence. He feels like a proud parent delighting in a child's belief in Santa Claus, remembering the time he too believed in such magic. Amos starts to think of the subway people as the innocents: the ones who can ride the trains without ever thinking about the things that have laid themselves down on the tracks. These thoughts make Amos feel almost ebullient, and when a few people sneak sideways glances in his direction, Amos realizes he may have laughed aloud.

When Amos arrives home, he enters through the side door, and the smell of sizzling bacon fat crawls inside his nose. When he reaches the kitchen, Lola turns from the pan to greet him but stops short when she sees his expression. "What's wrong, Mo-Mo?" she asks.

Amos tries to answer, but all he manages to say is "No."

He lurches forward, turns off the element, and retreats upstairs to escape the sizzle and stink.

Lola follows Amos into the bathroom and sits on the toilet while he takes another shower. She wants answers, but Amos does not provide them. Amos knows Lola to be a deep-feeling person. He is not convinced she can handle the things he wants to tell her: the blob, how it had glistened, trembled, and almost seemed to speak, how he had suspected the blob was connected somehow to his dad and was trying to communicate something. Amos decides to stay silent and keep Lola safe from the images that have crept inside his mind. Lola, Amos tells himself, is an innocent.

Amos turns up the hot water and raises his face to receive its scalding torrent. He sees his dad's face as if they are both underwater. The images are fleeting and distorted with brief flashes of clarity. Amos remembers the motion of his dad's elegant finger as it twirled a wedding ring against the soft edge of his thumb. He remembers a poem about raindrops. Amos cannot recall the poem's exact words, but he can hear his dad's lyrical voice reading the lines aloud in his mind. Amos imagines a raindrop, a clear, overfilled balloon with a miniature version of the whole word reflected on its surface. He imagines the raindrop quivering, vulnerable yet whole, locked in its descent in those precious seconds before it crashes into the ground.

The shower water goes cold, and Amos pulls back the curtain. He blinks into the steam of the room and realizes, with some relief, that Lola has gone.

When he wakes up later that afternoon, Amos boards the westbound subway. His mother lives in a condo down by the lakeshore, and although she has not invited Amos to visit, he knows Eunice will want to hear about his first day on the job. Eunice has been tight-lipped, but Amos suspects she is the only reason they accepted him into the police force. He did not score particularly well on his entrance exams.

Eunice never comes to Amos's house. She thinks Lola is a flake who's got her head stuck so far up her ass she can smell her own breath backward. Lola never calls Eunice by her name; she just calls her Sergeant Vader and has programmed Amos's phone to play "The Imperial March" whenever his mother calls.

When Amos arrives at Eunice's condo, he finds his mother in the living room, watching KPX-24 *Crime Scene* on her big screen. Eunice does not rise to acknowledge Amos. Her eyes remain fixed, as always, on the screen and the silent scenes across the city that she can no longer attend following Donna Tran's treachery.

Amos imagines how Eunice must have watched him last night, willing him not to blow it, but somehow knowing that he would. He remembers how he had stood shivering before the cameras and willed himself to be still, how he turned his face sideways to show his mother the hard angle of his jaw, the only part of him that doesn't look like his dad's, the only part of him that doesn't ask her to remember.

Amos sits beside Eunice on the couch. A box of reheated chicken wings rests between them, and Eunice drags a slick, orange morsel against the congealing edges of the cardboard.

"That little shit is going to look at the body. Just wait," Eunice says as she points a well-picked bone toward the screen.

Amos looks to the screen, sees Leon Martin, a fellow newbie, and says a silent thanks to the universe for the close-up shot on screen. The limited field of view prevents Amos from scanning the sidewalk for brain blobs. Amos notes how in control Leon looks, and it gives him hope, but as the camera zooms out, the orange sheet comes into view. Amos tries to focus on Leon's face and lets the rest of the picture blur around it. Leon presses his lips together, he flicks his eyes toward the camera, and they drop.

Eunice hurls her chicken bone at the television and hollers, "Goddamn, boy, that's just the shot they were waiting for!" She turns to Amos and says, "They always want to make us look like turds."

Amos inhales deeply of the stale condo air as Eunice shifts her body to face him. He presses his toes against his boot soles. He can tell Eunice has sensed a disturbance in the Force.

"Why weren't you on that scene after ten, Amos?" she says. She leans in closer, as if she can smell the shame that has begun to creep across his skin. "Zimmy said you were on till seven. You should have been guarding that body all night."

Amos thinks of how he had been unable to stand the scrutiny of the zoom lenses and the sinister way they whispered for him to look at the body. Amos thinks of the four times total he had vomited in the homicide van and how, when he had come out the last time, Sergeant Tran had asked him if he'd mind being assigned to a disturbance that had just been called in from the subway.

"Tran reassigned me to another scene," Amos says, but he knows Eunice's huntress eyes are seeing through the trees.

"Why would she do that?" Eunice inquires, her voice as gentle as a blade's unsheathing.

Amos mumbles an inadequate explanation but knows it doesn't matter what he says. Eunice has always been able to read his mind. Suddenly he is back in the fifth grade, face down on the soccer field, listening to the boom of Eunice's voice as it hammers in from the stands.

"Get the hell up, goddamn you, and finish the job. Toughness is a state of mind."

Amos selects a chicken wing from the box and avoids Eunice's eyes. He abandons his original plan to subtly ask his mother how she'd managed to deal with things when she first started on the job. He realizes he's caught himself just in time. Eunice is a woman and a single parent to boot, but she still made sergeant. She hadn't climbed that high by being soft-hearted. That much Amos should know.

Amos looks at Eunice's nose and notices how a few more of the capillaries beneath her skin have burst. He wonders if she is drinking more and if she ever gets lonely by herself in the condo.

When Eunice catches Amos looking, she hisses, "What the fuck is your problem, Amos?" and all he can think of to say is, "I hardly know."

Amos discovers there is truth to what Sergeant Tran said, and things do get easier. There is something reassuring about the groupthink, the way the force can enact things as a unit. Amos finds places to hide himself within the machine. If he hesitates, there is usually a more enthusiastic hand than his to press a teen-ager's flesh to a wall or bellow at a screaming mother that there's nothing the police can do about the choices her son makes. Amos makes himself the "read them the rights" officer, the one who fills out all the paperwork, the one who opens the cruiser door while his comrade throws a thrashing man-child inside. By learning to creep along the rim, Amos maintains a steady boil, but the froth never leaves the pot.

Not every shift produces a body, and when the bodies do come, Amos learns to ignore them and bury things deeper. He makes jokes like "I love the smell of fresh decomp in the morning" and "Hey, brother, can you lend me a hand?" and from the outside, at least, he is just another one of the tough dogs.

One day, during shift change, Amos meets Leon Martin coming out of a McDonald's washroom. The smell of vomit lingers between them, and Amos tells Leon about the time he too vomited in the forensics van. He doesn't finish the story because Leon laughs and says, "Woah, buddy, too much information." Amos accommodates for his miscalculation by pretending to vomit in Leon's coffee, and they both snort like tusked hogs.

Amos continues to vomit in the city's various toilets, but his weak constitution does not get the better of him. He always gets right back out on the pavement. Whenever Amos feels he might slip underwater, he thinks of Sam Spade, his smooth voice and commanding presence, and tries to channel them. The vision of

Spade becomes so prominent in Amos's mind that he sometimes feels like he might actually transform into the man himself. Not detective Spade, but early years Spade, while he was still walking the beat. Amos starts to hope that after a few years, he too might make detective. He imagines how it would feel to have Lola run her warm hands along the inside lining of his slippery grey trench coat.

Lola tells Amos she is worried about his nightmares and wonders aloud if he is "going off the deep end." Amos often has dreams that cause him to call out, rise from his bed, and sleepwalk through their bedroom. He tells Lola the dreams are nothing new, and although this is technically true, they both know things are getting worse.

Lola tries to convince Amos to go back to his old job working security at the General, but Amos tells himself not to listen. He thinks of Eunice, how she watches him on KPX-24 *Crime Scene*. He imagines her reaction if he makes detective.

Eventually, Lola refuses to leave things alone and suggests that Amos talk to her friend who is studying psychotherapy. Amos resists. He does not want to talk to anyone about the vomit, the blob, and all the other things he cannot un-see. He is afraid if he lets these things creep too close to the surface, he will not be able to stop them from emerging and staining everything he touches, including Lola. Amos prefers to let Sam Spade run the show, and for Amos – Puke-Amos, Face-Down-on-the-Soccer-Field-Amos, Look-at-the-Body Amos – to recede into a tiny raindrop and dissolve into the mud.

Eventually, Amos notices that Lola doesn't call him Mo-Mo anymore; she only ever calls him Amos.

"Amos, are you listening to me?"

"Amos, how much have you had to drink tonight?"

"Amos, I don't know who the fuck you are anymore."

Amos decides this is the price he must pay to protect Lola, to allow her to remain an innocent. He feels proud of himself for keeping things under control. He starts to sleep nights on the couch, so Lola won't hear him yelling. Some nights, when the sleep will not come, he sits in his living room and tries to remember how his life used to be before he saw the things that cannot be unseen. He remembers Friday night porch beers and how Lola would read him Green Lantern comics from her dad's collection before they went to bed. He remembers the feel of her mouth on his chest in the nighttime, how sometimes she'd kiss his skin while she was almost asleep. The more time passes, the more Amos feels like that former life happened to someone else.

Occasionally, Lola still comes down to the couch to sit with Amos, and when it becomes clear he is not up for chatting, she turns on one of her films and watches it beside him in silence. Amos no longer watches the films. Instead, he soothes himself with the vision of the screen's soft glow on Lola's face, the way the actor's images dance across the surface of her eyes. It occurs to Amos that life can be beautiful as long as he holds himself inside a dream and lets the sinister things hover just outside of his perception. On Lola's screen, Mary Astor tells Sam Spade she doesn't care what his secrets are, and Amos smiles. It reassures him he is doing the right thing.

Six months after he joins the force, Amos goes to 36 Division for his first 360 evaluation. As he approaches the building, "The Imperial March" plays from inside his pocket. When Amos answers the phone, Eunice says, "Watch what you say to that dipshit. Don't give her an inch. If you show her any part of it, she'll bite your entire ass."

As he nears the door, Amos raises his cupped palm, blows against it, and the reassuring smell of spearmint drifts backward from his fingers.

The detectives surround the Keurig machine and as he passes them, Amos raises his hand in greeting. He then stops to admire the crisp line of trench coats draped across the hooks beside the homicide door. One of the detectives says, "Brain fart or something, Brownlea?" and Amos realizes he is close to a fumble, so he trudges forward.

When Amos arrives in Sergeant Tran's office, he sits on the cracked vinyl chair across from her desk. Tran smiles, and her perfect teeth glisten. "That shit-eating grin of hers," Amos hears Eunice say.

Amos listens as Sergeant Tran reviews his mediocre but passable performance and tries to look enthusiastic when she makes suggestions for his improvement. The review reaches its natural conclusion, and Sergeant Tran leans back her chair. She says, almost as an afterthought, "I'll tell you, Brownlea, there was pressure from some avenues not to hire you, with all your family has been through. Your mother asked me specifically to keep quiet on it and tell the rest of the officers to do the same. So, I hope you haven't had any problems."

Amos feels a shadow enter the room but stays silent. He wills Sergeant Tran not to mention his dad.

"I'm glad to see you've generally made a success of yourself," Tran says.

Amos does not respond, so Sergeant Tran eases her elbows forward on her desk and continues.

"Off the record, Brownlea, how're things? Everything okay on the home front?"

Many things trickle toward the edges of Amos's lips, but he does not say them. Part of him longs to tell Sergeant Tran about the blob, the bacon, and the dreams. He wants to tell her how, when they identify the body and the family comes screaming, he can barely stand it and sometimes wishes it was him beneath the orange sheet. But Tran is a snake, and Amos knows he cannot trust her, so the things that want out stay in.

"That first night with the homicide and the jumper," Sergeant Tran says, "I thought you might lose your cookies, but you held it together. A couple of the guys thought I should have pulled you right away, you know, because of your dad."

Amos feels a thousand doors slam shut in his mind, and he rises from his chair.

"We done here, Sergeant?" Amos says.

"Sure, Brownlea, we can be. But I wondered if you might be willing to talk it out with me a little?"

"I'd rather not, if it's all the same," Amos says. By the time Sergeant Tran replies, he is already out the door.

That night, even after eight shots of Bushmills, Amos cannot fall asleep. He creeps up the stairs and slides into his old place in bed beside Lola. When he wakes up, he finds himself standing beside the open balcony door with the cold night air rushing around him. Amos hears Lola yelling, and he realizes he has been sleep-walking. He brings his hand up because his cheek feels like it is on fire.

"Had to slap you six times before you woke up enough to come inside," Lola hollers. "What the fuck, Amos? I thought you were gonna go over the goddamn rail."

"Maybe not such a bad idea," Amos says before he can stop himself, and then tries to laugh it off. The laugh doesn't work, and soon all Amos can hear is the sound of Lola's shouting. She tells him he's carving up his insides and she doesn't know why. She asks him who the hell he thinks would want to live with a younger version of goddamn Eunice? Amos's dad flashes into his mind, and he says, "Who, indeed?"

The next day, Amos comes home from work and finds Lola watching KPX-24 *Crime Scene* with red-rimmed eyes and a mostly empty six of Bud. When he comes to stand beside her, Lola looks up and says, "I don't get it, Amos. What happens here that fucks you up like this? It's just a bunch of assholes standing around, filling out forms, and getting rained on."

"How long you been watching this crap?" Amos tries to keep the fear from his voice.

"All day long, just like fuckin' Sergeant Vader," Lola says and starts to cry. "It feels like it's the only time I can even see you anymore, the only time you aren't hiding yourself from me."

A torrent of words gather in Amos's throat and block the sound of his voice from escaping. Amos slams the laptop shut and hears a sickening shatter. Lola opens the laptop, sees the ruined screen, and says, "Perfect, Amos, just fucking perfect."

Amos stares at the screen's jagged pattern, and many things come into his mind, but he does not say them. He just tells Lola to relax and he will take the computer to Staples after his shift because he's pretty sure it's still under warranty.

Midway through his shift, Amos walks through the Rouge Valley Urban Park with Zimmermann, one of the older detectives. It is a long way back to the body, so the two of them talk as they trudge.

"You're Eunice's kid," Zimmerman says, and Amos nods. "A fucking shame about your dad, Brownlea. I was on the day he went over."

Amos has difficulty attending to the detective's words. He feels something tighten beneath his sternum, and Sam Spade says, "Yeah. Mom's done alright."

The detective stands still, looks at Amos straight on, and Amos can feel him detecting.

"Any son of hers is bound to be a trooper, I guess," the detective says.

"I'm a hell of a guy," says Sam Spade.

"Your mom," says Zimmermann, "is the toughest woman I know. It was her first year on the job. What were the chances she would get the call for him? We thought it was just another jumper."

Sam Spade smiles his wry smile and says, "They're all just another jumper, Zimmermann."

"I guess," Zimmerman says, and although he nods, his expression is hard to read. "Jesus. If she had said something, we would have pulled her off, but she just – "

"Filled out the paperwork. An unidentified male." Sam Spade says and flicks the rim of his invisible fedora.

"Do you think she did it on purpose?" Zimmermann asks. "Was she afraid what we'd say? It was two weeks before we got a positive ID from your aunt."

Amos concentrates on his breathing, keeps it even and measured. A multitude of things pulse through his head all at once. He wants to slam his mind shut, but there are too many boots jammed in the door: Zimmermann's questions, Tran's probing, Lola's proximity to danger, and the path before him that can only lead to the sight of another nameless body.

"I asked her about it later," Zimmermann continues. "Know what she said? Said she didn't recognize him. He was a mess there on the sidewalk, but you figure she must have known, right? His clothes? His hair? His ring?"

Amos has heard enough but finds he cannot compel his mouth to protest. Zimmermann continues talking, but Amos no longer hears him. He already knows the story the detective is telling. A crack appears in the clouds of his mind, and Amos remembers sitting with his seven-year-old ear to a closet wall, eavesdropping. The voice of his aunt Jayda says, "But why the hell didn't you say something?" and Eunice replies, "That thing on the pavement had nothing to do with my husband. That thing on the pavement was an unidentified male."

Amos feels the detective's stare start to niggle through his scalp.

"Jesus, Brownlea. I'm sorry. I shouldn't be saying any of this to you. It's just that when I saw you coming across the field there, it all kinda came rushing back. You look like him, do you know that?

Shit. I guess I shouldn't mention that either, right? What can I say, Brownlea? It's nothing compared to what Eunice went through, but it was traumatic for me too, in a way. Something I kept seeing again and again in my mind, you know?"

"Well, sir, she never talks about it much," Amos says, and that pretty much ends things.

The body is lying in a nest of tall grass, but Amos pays it no mind. He fixes his attention, instead, on a caterpillar as it inches its way up Amos's pant leg. He watches how it undulates like a tiny, tireless wave, and wonders if his own head is the creature's final destination. Amos wonders what his brain looks like, nestled beneath his navy toque and solid skull. Amos raises his hand and knocks timidly on the side of his forehead. He tries to analyze the vibration, transform it into an image he can comprehend.

Zimmerman calls, "Everything okay, Brownlea?" and Amos knows the answer to this question is "No," but he simply folds his arms in front of him and laughs.

"Just making sure it's still there," Amos says.

Zimmermann's brow furrows, but then his face relaxes, and he gives Amos the thumbs up.

Amos is crossing the 36 Division parking lot when "The Imperial March" pulses from his pocket. Eunice's voice sounds distant as she asks Amos to come to the condo as soon as he can.

"What's the matter, Ma?"

Eunice's voice takes on a desperate edge as she sputters, "Jesus Christ, can you just get your ass over here?"

Amos bounds past Sergeant Tran, who is entering her Honda.

"Anything wrong?" Sergeant Tran calls, and Amos quickens his pace so he can disappear into the street before she thinks to follow.

When Amos arrives at the condo, he finds Eunice lying on the foyer tiles. Eunice's stillness is unsettling, but the presence of death does not yet seem to be in the room. When Amos crouches beside her, he notices the persistent rise and fall of Eunice's chest and exhales. Amos looks back at Eunice's face and realizes she has opened her eyes.

"What the hell, Amos?" she says and sends a blast of her Jack Daniel's breath into the air between them. "I'm not fucking dead. Help me up and stop staring at me like a goddamn dope."

Amos considers the unnatural angle of Eunice's left leg and thinks better of helping her up.

"We'll need the medics, Ma. I think you've broke your hip."

"What are you a fuckin' doctor now, Amos?"

Amos pulls out his cellphone and starts to dial 911, but Eunice digs her nails into his forearm.

"You do what I say, Amos, and never mind the medics. Stop being so goddamn useless."

Amos puts his hands to his eyes, rocks back on his heels, and sits on the floor beside Eunice.

"Oh God. Oh God. Oh God," he mutters.

Eunice releases her grip and presses her sandpaper fingertips to his forearm.

"Steady now, Amos. Push it back," Eunice says.

Amos presses his hands harder into his skull, and his eyeballs start to shiver beneath their lids.

"What do we do when the bad thoughts come?" Eunice whispers in a familiar tone.

"We push them back," Amos says.

"Do we let them overtake us, Amos?"

"Never."

"What do we do?"

"We crush them."

"Yes?"

"And we carry on."

"Good. Now open your eyes, Amos. Do what you need to do."

Amos opens his eyes.

"Okay, okay, okay," Amos says to the wall behind Eunice's head. He gathers his hair in large handfuls and squeezes hard.

"You are an officer of the law, Amos, not some kid. You've handled worse without letting the bad stuff free."

Eunice holds forward her hands and waits for Amos to lift her.

Amos knows he should call 911, but if he does this, it won't be long before Eunice's condo is filled with paramedics, police, and firefighters – many of whom will recognize her as the former sergeant.

"I'm gonna call Sergeant Tran," Amos says.

"Amos, don't you fucking dare."

Amos enters the living room and paces, trying to hear his own thoughts over the sound of Eunice's hollering. He assembles the facts in his mind and hopes they will point him toward some sort of solution.

He thinks of Sergeant Tran and how despite what Eunice has said, she's the only person who has asked Amos how he's doing since this whole goddamn mess began. She is the only one, apart from Zimmerman, who hasn't treated him as if he were their mascot or some vaguely amusing joke. He thinks of Eunice lying broken in the foyer and considers the many people in her life to whom she has presented limited options.

He picks up his cellphone and dials Sergeant Tran.

"Brownlea?"

"Yeah. Listen, Mom needs an ambulance here at the condo, but I don't want everyone else to show up, you know? Just the medics, okay?"

"Brownlea, are you two in some kind of trouble?"

"Yeah. I guess so. In a lot of ways, really. But what's going on right now is I think Mom's broken her hip."

"Oh shit, Brownlea – "

"Yeah, and Sergeant, she's not at her best right now, you know? I feel like it's none of everyone's business … "

"I got you, Brownlea. How about I'll just call the back line and request a single crew only? Then I'll get in the cruiser and come – "

"Sergeant?"

"Yeah, Brownlea?"

"I'm thinking you might be one of the prime people she doesn't want to see right now."

There is a long pause on the line, and a feeling creeps over Amos that he has made a mistake.

"Brownlea?

"Yeah?"

"She'll never tell you this, so I will. You are a good person."

Amos is not sure what to say, so he stays silent.

"I'll get the medics," Sergeant Tran says.

While they wait in the emergency room for the surgeon, Amos sets his cracked laptop on Eunice's stretcher so she can watch the KPX-24 *Crime Scene*. Leon Martin stares forward across the night sky and never once looks at the body.

"He's getting better," Eunice says. "Not perfect. But better."

Together they watch the yellow tape flutter, the steam swirl above the sewers, and eventually, Amos falls into a fitful sleep in his chair.

Amos finds himself upright when he awakens, staring at the stained surface of a hospital curtain as a nurse rushes forward to ask if everything is okay. Amos feels confused, but Eunice is quick to answer. "It's fine," she says, "He always gets nightmares, but he wakes up quick."

When the nurse has gone, Eunice stares at Amos in the half-light of the bluescreen.

"I was always scared shitless of how much you were like him," Eunice says. "What it meant about you."

"I know, Ma," Amos says, "I'm sorry."

It is early morning by the time Amos returns home, and Lola is still sleeping. He sits on the edge of their bed and watches the sunlight reflect off Lola's forehead. Lola's hair spills over the side of the bed, and Amos kneels to press her locks between his fingers. He brings the hair close to his nostrils and inhales the soapy aroma of her shampoo. He follows the scent trail upward, and when he reaches Lola's scalp, he presses his face against her skin and tries to breathe his wife inside of him.

Lola startles awake and sits up in the bed.

"Amos, what the fuck are you doing?"

Amos does not answer. He walks into the bathroom and turns on the shower. By the time Amos realizes he is still wearing his uniform, the water has already soaked through to his skin.

Lola pulls back the curtain tells Amos he is screwed in the head, that he is scaring her now and has gone too far. She needs him to talk to her. No, more than that, she needs him to get some real professional help. She is afraid to live with him the way he is. She is never sure what he will do next. Amos notices that fear has coated Lola like thick oil, and he realizes he has failed her, that he has infected her, that she is starting to see the unseeable.

Amos walks out of the shower, straight past Lola, and descends the stairs.

There are only six hours left before he starts his next shift, so he walks the thirty kilometres to 36 Division. By the time he gets there, he is only half an hour early, and his uniform is almost completely dry.

Sergeant Tran comes out of her office to ask him how everything went with Eunice, and Sam Spade says, "Just fine, Sergeant, just fine." He shakes Sergeant Tran's hand, smiles an old Hollywood smile, and presses Amos back underground.

Amos drives out to another Queen Street scene and changes the guard with Leon Martin. Leon gives him a fist pump and tells him, "Looks like we got ourselves another jumper." Amos doesn't bother to ask the story of the person lying beside him under the orange sheet. He's decided to be no longer interested in the troubles of strangers.

The KPX-24 crew is already in position, and Amos listens to the sounds of their camera lenses flexing as they try to get the best possible shot of his face. Amos thinks about Eunice in her hospital bed with her new hip and his broken laptop. He turns his face sideways, hardens his jaw, and does not look at the body.

The coroner arrives on scene. She looks very young, though if she's already a doctor, she must be at least twenty-five. She seems nervous and smiles a lot as she circles the perimeter of the orange sheet. She pulls a body tag from her clipboard and starts to fill in the lines. Amos does not need to look at the tag. He knows what the coroner is writing. There is no family weeping in the alleyway or standing in a sad circle beside the forensics van, so as the coroner's marker squeaks across the moist surface of the tag, the letters fall across Amos's mind like fresh snow: *unidentified male.*

The coroner kneels beside the body and eases back the orange sheet just far enough to reveal a frozen finger.

"I don't think anyone really needs to see the whole mess," the coroner says. "He's going in for post-mortem anyway, right?"

She gives Amos a hesitant wink, and Amos is about to let it slide, but then it occurs to him that he is not the only one in this world who needs to get tougher.

Suddenly Sam Spade comes out to play. "Whatever you say, doctor, but most coroners have the stomach for at least a quick look."

A glimmer of shame creeps over the coroner's face, and she exhales in a slow, steady stream. "It's not the body really," she says. "Just, the scene, the – mess."

Amos would like to tell the coroner he knows precisely what she means and is wondering, at this very moment, what would happen if he just laid himself down on the ground beside her and let everything inside him spill out over the street. But Sam Spade just smiles, rests his hand on the coroner's shoulder, and says, "It'll be okay, doc, one day this won't even touch you."

A lake breeze drifts in, and the body tag flutters like an autumn leaf. Fog creeps out from the alley, and the yellow tape sways. The faint drizzle surrounding them turns to wet snow, and then the screaming starts.

A detective's distant voice says, "Looks like we got our positive ID." Another one chuckles and says, "In all the years I've heard them screaming, it's never brought one of them back."

Amos thinks of how Eunice's body looked as it lay in the foyer and the coldness in Lola's eyes when he had told her he was leaving. He imagines the stillness of his own body pressed against the pavement, how the orange sheet would fail to contain him. It occurs to Amos that soon there will be nobody left to scream for him in the alleyway, that maybe he'll remain unidentified forever.

Amos looks toward the KPX-24 cameras and wonders if anyone is still watching. He wraps his palms around his toque, but it is too late. He feels the brain blobs start to trickle out his ears, his eyes, his throat.

Amos steps past the body and walks, entranced, toward the largest KPX-24 camera. He focuses on the glass centre of its lens and tries to see the world beyond it. He imagines the face of the woman he hopes still waits there, asks her, with his eyes, to help him.

Amos feels as if he is racing toward the water's surface, trying to reach it before he gasps for air. His cellphone plays "The Imperial March," but Amos ignores it, and eventually, the phone falls silent.

The cameraperson says, "Hey, buddy, hey. We're all just trying to do our job here … " and backs toward the news van.

Amos has almost reached the edge of the camera's lens when he hears the theme song he's been waiting for. The first bars of his favorite Kinks song cut through the falling snow, and Sam Spade tells Amos not to answer.

But he does.

Amos brings his hands to his eyes and wipes away the spatter of tiny droplets that have collected there, sends them to crash against the wet street.

There is only one thing left in the darkness that Amos can hear: the sound of Lola's voice.

"Mo-Mo? Mo-Mo?"

Amos looks at the camera and speaks to the woman behind the lens.

"I'm here," he says. "Lola, I'm here."

Ride the Reaper

This is exactly what friggin' happened. Every word's the truth.

I'm sitting at the table reading an ad in the paper for Hell-nail's Ride the Reaper tour, trying to figure out where me and Keith could scam the cash for a ticket, when Mom comes into the kitchen and tells me I'm kicked out of the apartment. It's all over some story Frank sold her about me being the kingpin of that fire down at the arena – not like he's got any proof. The kicker is, this is Culdafik Bay, where you're a wuss if you get your parka out before we hit minus thirty, so if I'm gonna be curb-surfing in the middle of February, I know I better get something going quick if I don't wanna end up bear bait.

There's no love lost between Mom and Gramps – took me till I was ten to realize his actual first name was Spike and not Goddamn – so I figure I'll swing by his place first. Gramps comes to the door of his trailer and goes, "You're a little shit, Stu, whole town knows it, but so am I. You treat me decent and I'll have your back. Won't ask you no questions, but that deal's gonna have to be reciprocal."

Gramps lets me sleep in the bedroom. Says he mostly takes the recliner anyway, on account of his rotten lungs. He tells me he's going down to the Fort in the morning to catch the Hellnail show and I can come with if I want to because his buddy left him hanging with an extra ticket.

The next day we drive six hundred clicks through a snow squall, slip into the Rock Swamp about eight seconds before Hellnail hit the stage, and it's worth every white-knuckled minute. The show is epic and I scream for two solid hours while Zoran Zotto rips up the stage. Black leather, pierced face, and tattoos from eyeballs to ass cheeks, Z flies out above the audience on a cable rig with his goddamn legs on fire and belts out the lyrics that become my creed:

"You gotta ride the reaper. Down. Down. Ride him through the ground till the devil wakes."

Z sings about darkness, hellfire, and all the thick muck that's churning underneath my own goddamn ribs. Our seats are so awesome that there's this one point where Z gets down real low to the stage and points his black fingernail right at me, so close I could almost touch it, and for the first time in as long as can I remember, I feel seen, like totally visible to another human being. I look over at Gramps and he's just swaying there beside me, half grinning, sorta muttering, and it doesn't matter that I can't hear his words. I know just what he's saying: "Friggin' A, man. Friggin' A."

Me and Gramps get along fine as roomies, just stay the hell out of each other's way mostly. Gramps is kinda like a four-foot-eight Clint Eastwood. He doesn't talk much, but when he does, you better listen good because whatever he says, it's gonna be crucial. One night after we catch the hockey on the tube, he leans over and goes, "Stu, you gotta stop screwin' around. Get a plan."

I know he's right. School is five years gone and I spend most of my time with Keith just kinda hanging around outside RadioShack, smoking, and giving people the gears. So, Keith gets this idea that we could sell some weed out behind the Legion and that works out fine, until it doesn't.

A few months into it, two cops bang on the door of the trailer with a warrant. I know there's about two pounds stashed in the bedroom closet, so when the one cop goes, "This yours, Stuart?" I figure I'm pretty well screwed. But then I hear Gramps's voice cut in from the doorway and he goes, "That there's mine. For my arthritis. You wanna take me down to the station, officer, I'll get my boots."

I can tell from the way the cop looks back and forth between me and Gramps that he's not buying it, but what the hell can he really say when Clint Friggin' Eastwood just told him that there's his weed? He pretty much has to go with it.

And he does.

On Gramps's second day in the slammer, he falls and breaks his goddamn hip. At first, I think he must've got in a fight with some juiced-up gangster in the jail yard; maybe got all "go ahead, make my day" and next thing you know – smash – it's blood drops bouncing off the hard-packed snow. Turns out he just slipped on some water in the cafeteria, but I guess the judge felt sorry for the old boy because he went ahead and suspended the sentence. So, with only two days served, Gramps went free.

So just when I think we're golden, Gramps gets a bit squirrelly after the operation to fix his hip. He's not completely bonkers, but just enough gone to let Mom take control of the whole situation and throw him in the White Moose Lodge nursing home. Then Keith hears from some guy up at the drive-through that they aren't letting Gramps have his smokes because they have him on some crap called the Prevention Pathway, and brother, there's just some shit you can't let stand.

Mom puts me on the no-fly list at the front desk of the Moose because by then Frank's got his hooks right into her about my being a bad influence and everything. When I cruise by with Gramps's smokes, I have to go around back and chuck the carton up to his second-floor balcony. Gramps was never a chatty dude at the best of times, but once he's locked up at the Moose, it gets so he won't talk to me at all, even if I bring him du Maurier Specials. I get pretty torn up about it, but I tell myself he's just out of his friggin' mind now and then try not to think about all the legit reasons he might have for giving me the high-hat.

One time I go by with the goods and he's up there staring out at the poxy moon like he's some kind of werewolf and he goes, "Wasn't trying to off myself, Stu, despite what your mother tells you. Just came out for a drag and the door froze shut. I hollered out but everyone was downstairs, so I just lay down and thought, 'Spike, you'll likely die of hypothermia before the smokes run out, so there's worse ways.'"

I don't know what the hell he's talking about, since Mom would sooner converse with the ass-end of a horse than me these days, but it's the most he's said to me in months so I try to keep him rolling. "Good thing they found you, Gramps."

"If you say so."

I don't like the sound of that, so I scare up something to lighten the mood. "Hey, Gramps, remember when we drove down to see Hellnail in that friggin' blizzard?"

"Yeah."

"Get a load of this, they're comin' to Culdafik next month. Gonna play an outdoor concert right out on the frozen bay. How's that for hardcore? Minus forty and I bet Z will still find a way to set himself on fire."

Gramps doesn't say anything for a long time so I just sorta stand there freezing my ass off while I watch the little red comet of his cigarette bounce around in the moonlight. Just when I think I'm about to lose my left nut, he goes, "Stu?"

"Yeah, Gramps?"

"You gotta get me to that goddamn concert."

Keith says the best thing is to just bust in there and grab him, old-school style. So, the night of the concert, we "borrow" Frank's van and haul ass over to the Moose. Keith cruises inside to case the joint, I sit lookout on the hood of the van, and it's not long before this girl in a security uniform comes over to check me out. She looks solid, sorta like a She-Hulk type, and wears this purple eyeliner that makes her eyes look nice and catty. She catches me looking and goes, "You Stu Guichet?"

I get all nervous, for some reason, so I go, "Who's friggin' asking?"

She looks at me like I'm boring the hell out of her and goes, "Name's Twyla. Got your picture at the security desk, says you're not supposed to be here."

I'm just about to wow her with a slick comeback when Keith comes shooting out the main entrance with some jerk-off in a crew cut hot on his tail. Keith's not much of a runner so the guy catches him pretty quick, and next thing you know, he's got Keith in a half nelson. Keith starts shrieking like a goddamn parakeet, and if there's one thing I can't stand it's when folks mess with Keith, so I spark up fierce and take a run at numbnuts there. I'm just about to get the upper hand when I feel myself being lifted through the air and then Twyla's got me pinned to the side of the van while Crew Cut throws a tantrum about Keith screwing around in the "restricted zone." I struggle a bit and manage to fire off a few good lines at Crew, but then Twyla leans in beside my ear and goes, "Why'nt you get the frig outta here while you still can?"

I feel her hot breath on the side of my neck and it smells just like Juicy Fruit and Player's Lights. I start to feel dizzy and I look down at her giant fists, still clutching my jacket, and I'm sorta in a trance as I go, "Your hands are like two beautiful crabs."

We decide Crew Cut's not worth the grief, and as we fishtail out of the parking lot Keith goes, "That Twyla is some woman." I gotta agree with him on that one, but it's too much to think about when it's T minus twenty minutes till Z hits the ice stage and Gramps is still up there in his goddamn cage. I go, "We need a friggin' backup plan, Keith," and he goes, "Should've had that before we tried the first one."

I'm ready to rip into him but just then he looks in the back of the van and goes, "I got it, Stu. Turn this mother around."

So there's us, hunkered down in the woods behind the Moose, packing snow down on top of a piece of plywood we got from the back of Frank's van, and Keith starts going on about a fixer. So I go, "What the frig's a fixer?" and he goes, "You know, someone on the inside, to grease the goddamn wheels?" And he's right, our last plan would've worked fine if Crew Cut there hadn't been such a hero, but we are running seriously short on time. "We gotta roll, Keith. The present is friggin' now."

That's when we hear footsteps coming in from the direction of the Moose and I think, *Well, here's the part where the whole thing goes balls up*, but then Twlya hits the scene, fixes me with her feline eyes, and goes, "Guichet, why did you say that freaky crap about my hands?"

Since I've been trying my best to block that ace line out of my memory, I've got no ready answer so I go, "Dunno. Just something I was thinking about." I feel my heart sucker punch the back of my tongue as Twyla goes, "What's a person's fists got to do with friggin' crabs? Doesn't make any sense."

I look down at her gloveless hands and I gotta say, her fingers look pretty red – almost like a bunch of juicy claws from the All-You-Can-Eat Bucket O'Sea special at Salty Stephen's – but I don't say anything because all of a sudden it hits me how I am a failure at literally friggin' everything in my life. Next thing I know I start sorta crying, so I take a whole handful of snow and rub it all over my face so neither of those two arseholes can see my shitty tears.

Twyla must not notice because she just keeps right on talking.

"Spike's a good old guy. Riffs with me about the metal scene sometimes. Said he could die happy if he just saw Z rock the stage one last time … "

I try to take it all in, but Twyla's words run over me like a goddamn avalanche.

" … Told me you were the only one in his family who ever gave half a shit about him. Said I should maybe give you a go since you weren't near as much of a screw-head as folks give you credit for. He was kinda calling out for you when I found him out there frozen on his balcony."

The sound of the Hellnail roadies running the sound check rings in from the distant bay, but I'd sooner shit syphilis than interrupt Twyla.

Twyla jams her hands in her pockets, widens her stance like the cop did right before he asked me about the weed, and goes, "This is how it's gonna happen. In fifteen minutes, there'll be a small commotion in the front entrance involving the fire alarm. A lotta things might go unmonitored for a bit while we sort that out."

Keith gives her a nod and I know just what he's thinking: looks like we got us our fixer.

We cruise up behind Gramps's balcony with our snow-covered plywood strapped to the top of a sled we stole from the Bargain Shop. It takes a couple of tries, but eventually we land the board so one end rests on the top rail of Gramps's balcony and the other end digs into the snow at our feet. Snow slide of the friggin' century. Gramps is waiting up there in his parka, and he struggles up the side of the balcony rail just as the fire alarm starts to wail. The way he sways gives me the willies, but the old guy is tenacious, and then all of a sudden he's up there on top of the rail and the next second he's sliding down to us on the ground.

I'm glad we have the sled because I can tell from the way Gramps is puffing there's no chance he's gonna make it down to the bay's edge on his own steam. The great thing about parkas is you can't tell who the hell anyone is when the hood is up, so nobody even gives us a whiff as we pull Gramps down Princess Street. Like I said, Gramps is a bit of a shrimp, so everyone probably thinks we're just pulling some kid.

Turns out the whole friggin' town is out to get an eyeful of Hellnail, so we get stuck way up the hill and need our binoculars to even see the stage. Part way into the first set, Gramps starts to look a bit Smurf, so I go, "Hey, Gramps, maybe we should take you back."

He looks up at me with those Clint-y old eyes and goes, "Stu, I'm going in."

He holds up his beer like he's handing me his goddamn sword and then chucks himself forward on the sled.

We lose sight of him for a sec because the faraway sound of someone yelling my name grabs hold of my attention. I look down the hill and there's Mom chugging up toward us like a five-foot-nothing freight train, with old Frank bringing up the rear and hollering like a hound. I remember about the van and how it's still parked in the lot back at the Moose. I fish Frank's keys out from my pocket and chuck them in the snow beside me. Keith knows what time it is and he gives me a nod.

Can't prove it? Didn't friggin' happen.

Suddenly Frank and Mom disappear from view. The crowd parts like actual Moses-water and in the middle of it appears Gramps, whipping down that hill like the sled's on rails.

I know I should run after him, but I just stand there frozen – like, literally, they don't call this place Cold-As-Fuck Bay for nothing – and then I hear Mom's voice say, "Shit, is that goddamn Spike down there on the sled?"

When Gramps gets to the bay, some drunk dudes lift him up above the crowd and they start to volley him toward the stage. I put up my binoculars and there he is, one fist holding on tight to the front of the sled, the other one up in the air pumping in time with the drums.

I hand the binoculars to Mom and just as she's adjusting the focus, Frank starts up griping, so she tells him to stick a cork in it. When she gets an eyeful of Gramps, Mom goes, "What's he doing, Stu?"

I know she's already guessed the answer, but I say it anyway: "Riding the friggin' reaper."

"Jesus Christ," she says, but I can tell from the way she says it that she's just figured something out.

"Friggin' A," I say. "Friggin' A." And we both nod because there's nothing else left to say.

When Gramps falls down, I try not to think of him lying there broken up under everyone's feet. Instead, I think of a pair of gloves I saw in the Bargain Shop when we went in for the sled. They were salmon orange, fleece-lined, and size XL. I think hard about those gloves and wonder if they'd keep a person's hands warm if they happened to be out on their night rounds at the White Moose Lodge nursing home.

I'm not making a plan or anything.

Just thinking, is all.

Acknowledgements

I would like to thank the following for their support in publishing earlier versions of the following:

"Animals in Captivity," *The New Quarterly*, 2022

"The Many Coffees of Marissa," *Solemates and other stories-Scottish Arts Trust, 2023*

"Fingered," *Atticus Review*, 2019

"Return of the Waxwing," *New Delta Review, 2022*

"Class Party," *Westchester Review*, 2019

"Female Jockeys," *Against the Bar*, Regulus Press, 2019

"The Poets of Blind River," *Carter v. Cooper 9 Anthology*, Exile Editions, 2021

"Norma's Fire," *Talking About Strawberries All the Time*, 2020

"Madam and Yves," *Funny Pearls*, 2019

"Sheila's Mine," *Aesthetica Magazine*, 2019

"Birds of the Falls," *Hong Kong Review*, 2023

"The Poacher," *Riddle Fence*, 2023

"We All Become Our Mothers," *Mystery Tribune*, 2021

"The Witch's Tooth," *Cream City Review*, 2019

"Beneath the Pond," *Malahat Review*, 2020

"Bone Jacked," *Into the Void*, 2020

"Ride The Reaper," *Booth Magazine*, 202

Additional thanks to: Carmella, Eva, Graham, Leigh, and Andrew for their excellent collaboration with the editing and presentation of this manuscript. Eva for kitchen poetry kinship, Renee for patio lifelines and always making time, Leo for loving me dearly despite being "creeped out" by my writing, Orla for passing demons beneath the door, Oskar for always focusing on the positive, Mom for her stealthy pride, and Edgar for infinite things.

Kate Segriff (she/her) is a Toronto-based writer and filmmaker. Her work has been published in *Atlanta Review*, *The Malahat Review*, *Prism International*, and *Best Canadian Poets*, among others. Her short films have appeared in over 50 independent festivals worldwide. She has won the *Space and Time Magazine* Iron Writer Award, the *Pulp Literature* Bumblebee Prize for Flash Fiction, the Wilda Hearn Prize for Flash Fiction, the Connor Prize for Poetry and the Edinburgh Short Story Award.